About the

Susanne Huffman and Mindy Nix are mother-daughter French professors, business owners and lifelong Francophiles. They created their business, Oui & Sí, to share their love of language, travel and culture with others. When they aren't reading, writing or teaching, they are dreaming up their next trip to Paris together. They are both married to men who lovingly oblige their adoration of all things

French and are their biggest supporters in all of their endeavours.

Susanne has a son named Oliver who loves French music and *pain au chocolat*. Mindy has two grown children, Susanne and her brother, Doug, and three grandchildren whom she dreams of taking to France.

Jana,
Merci mon amie!
Je t'aime!

Mindy

THE FRENCH PROFESSOR

This is a work of fiction. Names, characters, businesses, places, events and incidents are either the products of the author's imagination or used in a fictitious manner. Any resemblance to actual persons, living or dead, or actual events is purely coincidental.

SUSANNE HUFFMAN AND MINDY NIX

THE FRENCH PROFESSOR

Vanguard Press

VANGUARD PAPERBACK

© Copyright 2022
Susanne Huffman and Mindy Nix

The right of Susanne Huffman and Mindy Nix to be identified as authors of this work has been asserted by them in accordance with the Copyright, Designs and Patents Act 1988.

All Rights Reserved

No reproduction, copy or transmission of this publication may be made without written permission.
No paragraph of this publication may be reproduced, copied or transmitted save with the written permission of the publisher, or in accordance with the provisions of the Copyright Act 1956 (as amended).

Any person who commits any unauthorised act in relation to this publication may be liable to criminal prosecution and civil claims for damages.

A CIP catalogue record for this title is available from the British Library.

ISBN 978 1 80016 406 2

Vanguard Press is an imprint of
Pegasus Elliot MacKenzie Publishers Ltd.
www.pegasuspublishers.com

First Published in 2022

Vanguard Press
Sheraton House Castle Park
Cambridge England

Printed & Bound in Great Britain

Dedication

For Poppy

Acknowledgements

We are deeply thankful to our wonderful people, including both immediate and extended family and friends who are like family. Everyone in our lives has shown us nothing but love and support, and for that we extend our most heartfelt gratitude.

Thank you to each person who has crossed our paths on this journey. Each of you has inspired a piece of our story and inspired us to write about what we know, learning, teaching, exploring, trying and failing, then trying again.

To Poppy, Mindy's husband and Susanne's father, thank you for insisting we accomplish our dream of writing a book in time to present it to you for your sixtieth birthday. We wouldn't be here without you.

Partie Un
La Flâneuse

Paris, France

Chapter 1

Margaret was not neurotic, at least not any more. Oh sure, she still had her quirks — flying made her palms sweaty and always would; she had to check several times to make sure the coffee pot was off before leaving her apartment; and she was always slightly worried about whether the server had washed their hands before handling her food — but as she sipped her Bordeaux at Café de la Paix, her favourite Sunday afternoon tradition since moving to Paris, she had an epiphany. She was still nervous sometimes, but the fear and crippling anxiety she used to live with had drifted away like the boats passing leisurely on the Seine. Perhaps it was one of the gifts of getting older, or the result of a series of small, but brave decisions she had made over the years. Whatever the cause, Margaret relished the peace she had finally found.

She had been here for years but still felt delighted and immensely thankful every morning when she rose and realized that this majestic city was her home. The City of Lights. She actually lived here. She loved everything about living in her neighbourhood, *le quartier latin*. It wasn't as chic as some of the other *arrondissements*, but she loved all the bookstores and cosy cafés nearby. Plus, there was a vibrancy of youth that surrounded her here and there always seemed to be a buzz of excitement and energy in the air. There was a university nearby, the Sorbonne, and as she watched the students hurry to and from class, Margaret liked to daydream that she was also in school there. She toyed with the idea of signing up for a class; she loved learning and thought it would be absolutely dreamy to walk the halls at the famed university. She smiled and dared to dream further. Maybe she would apply to teach a class there. *Pourquoi pas?* It was a really long shot, but she had the experience, and Margaret found that long shots often worked out when she simply put herself out there. Moving to France had been her most recent leap of faith. No one, herself included, would have believed that she would be living in Paris at the age of sixty-five.

She grinned as she recalled telling her children of her plans to sell her home and move to France. Her new place in Paris was nothing like her house back home. Her home in the States had been large compared to her new shoebox of an apartment. It had been nestled in a very nice quiet neighbourhood. There was a beautiful park nearby and trails for walking. But she had to walk a mile to get to her local coffee shop, and she couldn't just breeze out of her front door to grab groceries or a glass of wine. When she stepped out of her apartment door in Paris, there were endless places she could walk for *le petit déjeuner*. She didn't even own a car here. It was when she sold her car, she thought, that her family realized she meant business. She wasn't just spending a summer or even a year in Paris, she was moving and beginning a new chapter here.

Walking around the city was her absolute favourite thing to do and she went to bed pondering which little café she would visit the next morning for her *café crème*. She did have a coffee pot in her apartment for an early morning cup. She so enjoyed the familiar comfort of waking up to the smell of fresh coffee, so each night before bed she programmed it to brew at six a.m. sharp. Her beloved coffee maker was one of three miniscule appliances in her new home. It was joined by a small toaster oven and an even smaller refrigerator, which looked like it belonged in a dorm room, not a grown woman's apartment.

Her family thought she could have done better when they first came to visit and saw the place. It was on the third floor and although there was an elevator, or *un ascenseur*, it only held one person and she was terrified of getting stuck in it. Few residents used it and she imagined herself trapped there for days before anyone noticed. So she took the stairs and considered it her exercise. The apartment itself looked more like a room in a bed and breakfast than an entire home. It was all one room, her bed, which she covered with a luxurious white bedspread she had found at Galeries Lafayette; a table and two chairs, which she had scoured the Marché aux Puces for; and a small sofa that had come with the apartment, which sat in front of a wall of bookshelves.

She had brought only her most favourite books, the top twenty, which had taken up precious suitcase space but were so worth it. She wanted to fill the rest of the bookshelf space with new favourite books from France. Mostly books written in French, of course. The French had written most of the classics that she loved. Alexander Dumas' *The Count of Monte Cristo*, Victor Hugo's *Les Misérables* and *The Hunchback of Notre Dame,* and Jules Verne's *Journey to the Centre of the Earth* were at the top of her list. She had already added one, Peter Mayle's *A Year in Provence*. It was in English but was so utterly charming that she made an exception.

Charming was, in fact, how she would describe the little room in which she lived. There were odd little angles everywhere, which her daughter, Claire, found delightful but her son, Joseph, did not, especially after he hit his head on one of them in the bathroom. The apartment had one large window that opened up onto a faux balcony, where she could let the breeze in on nice days.

The bathroom, though impractical, was divine. It consisted of an ornate pedestal sink that didn't hold so much as a toothbrush (every one of her toiletries had to fit in the tiny medicine cabinet behind the mirror), a toilet, and a clawfoot tub. The tub doubled as her shower, although she had to bend down slightly to wash her hair since the showerhead was so short. Everything was so petite yet well made, and she often imagined that a very small yet stylish French woman must have owned it before her. Margaret was so thankful to have a tub to soak in, which was still her favourite evening ritual in Paris. Her bathroom had a little skylight, and when she was relaxing in the bath, she could see the stars twinkling, or often, the rain softly falling.

The feature that had really sold her on the apartment, though, was the little staircase that led to a loft above her kitchen. It was just large enough to fit a full-size mattress, an oversized chair and a lamp, meaning she could actually have guests. She topped the bed with a comfortable duvet and extra blankets, then added a small rug to make the space cosy. Rachel and Jill were set to visit soon, and the thought of them trying to climb the tiny set of stairs after too much wine made her giggle. Her kids had promised to come often as well, although the one who enjoyed the little loft space the most was her cat, George II.

Her children thought it was slightly morbid that she would name him after her previous beloved pet, who had passed away a few years earlier after a wonderfully long life, but Margaret thought the name was actually quite regal. He was a European cat, after all. They kept asking her if she was lonely, would she also like a dog for company? *Absolument, non.* It was true that George II was not George the original. He was a French cat, after all, and he took his time warming to new people, but he was always waiting for her to come home and he loved to sleep under the covers next to her. She and George II spoke French but she was teaching him a bit of English because it was important to be bilingual. George II provided her just the kind of company she needed. Besides, the whole city kept her company, and she slept soundly at night listening to the hum of traffic and George II's murmured purrs.

She could have afforded something a bit nicer, but she loved this quirky building set right in the middle of this equally quirky neighbourhood. She had experienced enough normal to last a lifetime. The freedom of finally dressing, talking, eating, *living* exactly how she liked was so liberating.

Cooking was slightly tricky. There was basically just one small counter in her kitchen. On one end was her toaster oven, coffee pot and a stove with just one burner. The world's most petite sink sat on the other end. In between there was about a foot of prep space, but she had the most beautiful butcher block counters, and she could chop and knead right on top of them. Not that she did a lot of chopping and kneading. The *boulangers* were far better than she would ever be at making bread. She did like to prepare herself a warm dinner at home on a freezing night, but what made cooking here particularly difficult was not her dollhouse of a kitchen, but that the *boulangers*, *bouchers* and *fromagers* were taking their time warming to her.

She also had to figure out all of the unspoken rules here, like the fact that the French didn't really stand in line, they just kind of pushed their way forward. The first time she went to buy cheese, she waited thirty minutes and had made no headway towards the front. She started watching the others and realized she was going to have to get aggressive. This was business, not personal. But once at the front, customers were expected to know what they wanted immediately, especially if they were not a regular. She noticed that some special customers got samples and advice about which cheese to pair with the veal they were serving that evening. But she only got frosty stares and curt questions. *"Qu'est-ce que vous voulez, madame?"* So, she took to frequenting the same *fromagerie* daily, hoping that her patience would pay off. It took several months of persistence before she was accepted, but the challenge made it feel like a real victory.

One day, quite unexpectedly, Monsieur Gérard asked her what she was having for dinner that night. She quickly made up an imaginary meal. "Oh, um, I'm thinking duck confit, monsieur." She had no concept of what duck confit even was, though obviously it involved the death of some poor duck. Really, she just wanted some cheese to go with her bread and wine. Her response must have been correct, however, because it was met with an, *"Oh, la la. Excellent choix, madame."* Monsieur Gérard got to work finding her the perfect *fromage.* "You need a subtle cheese to go with such a strong and robust meal. May I suggest the Camembert. Please, try a bite, it melts in your mouth." Margaret wondered why cheese in France was so much better than in the U.S. She thanked Monsieur Gérard for his help, trying not to let on just how delighted she was that he'd warmed to her.

Truthfully, the joy filled her head to toe as she left the *fromagerie* that day. She was making headway with the locals, and she enjoyed cooking with such fresh yet decadent ingredients. She did enjoy the ritual of preparing a meal, but unlike many, she had not come to Paris to cook. Attending the Cordon Bleu was not on her bucket list, even though she adored Julia Child. She had read *My Life and France* years ago and was utterly charmed by her story. But Margaret mostly preferred to bring her meals in, like crusty sandwiches with ham and cheese or a slice of melt in your mouth quiche. Sometimes she just ate cheese that her new friend the *fromager* had suggested that day, always accompanied by a baguette from the *boulangerie* and perhaps topped off with a macaron from Ladurée. How lucky she felt to have a Ladurée store close by. No, it was not the flagship store which, she told Claire one day on the phone, simply had to be seen in person. It was too beautiful to put into words. But hers was quaint and she loved that it was *hers*, like all of the shops and restaurants in her neighbourhood.

Her favourite pastime was dining out. That was the whole point; she wanted to be fully immersed in the city. The cafés were a big part of what made Paris, Paris. She was one of those people who was not self-conscious when eating alone. She was so absorbed in whatever book she had brought, that she was completely lost if indeed someone had been staring at her with pity. And after she had read a good while, she finished her meal with people watching, which was as good as going to the cinema, maybe better.

And of course, there were the bookstores. Oh, the glorious bookstores.

She loved going to Galignani because they had both French and English books, and mostly because the world-famous, Angelina, and their, *to die for* hot chocolate, was next door. It was so popular that they had it available at a darling little cart right outside the restaurant for anyone to pick up a cup to go. It was un-French actually to take your drink to go, but she was still an American, and sometimes she liked to hold a warm drink as she walked around on chilly days.

There was also the beloved Shakespeare and Company, the famous bookstore right across from Notre Dame. It had tiny rooms stuffed floor to ceiling with all different types of books and it was the kind of place where you always felt you would find just the one you were looking for. They actually let people live upstairs and for their rent, they just worked in the bookstore. Perhaps that could be a backup plan if she ran out of money. She'd probably work there for free in all honesty. There was at least one store cat and the entire environment was so warm. A café had been added to the bookstore and Margaret could think of no better afternoon than buying a novel and then sitting at the café. She was beyond content. She would have to take George II to visit. She was sure he was a book-lover. All good cats are.

George II was an orange cat just like George. He was huge and fluffy and got fur everywhere, but she forgave him because she loved him. Sometimes she showed him a picture of the original George because she thought George II should know about the history of his namesake. George II listened patiently and she appreciated his respect for the recently deceased.

Fortunately for Margaret, it was not hard at all to find a new batch of stray cats to take care of. Paris had cats everywhere. In fact, she found out that in France the cat is a more popular pet than a dog. But alas, there were still many strays. She no longer had to go out at night as she no longer had a real day job, so she was not frightened when she found some strays behind a boulangerie one day on a walk. It was obvious that the *boulanger* fed them from time to time, as they did not look starving, but they gobbled up the food she left and drank the water in a bowl she placed behind a dumpster. This was how, just weeks into her living in Paris, she came to meet and adopt George II. It wasn't difficult. She wasn't looking for a good-looking cat, she was looking for a cat that seemed to need her. Within a month, a humongous orange furry monster of a cat had dared to approach her and she knew he was the one.

Although he was friendly, he was still a bit skittish. She trod lightly, letting him come to her, and every day he warmed up to her a bit more. One month later he was sitting on her lap, purring and eating cat treats out of her hand. She felt a bit guilty, choosing this cat over the others, and hoped that they would not be jealous nor miss their street friend. But she brought him with her occasionally to visit and he stayed on her lap as if he feared she would leave him there. The other cats ignored him. They seemed not to recognize this fat cat.

Margaret's biggest fear was that her landlord would not allow pets, so she snuck him upstairs without asking permission. But she had worried needlessly; the landlord handed her a bite of cheese one day saying that all French cats like cheese. He turned out to be quite right. George II was a bit choosy about his cheese, though. He preferred stinky cheeses like Raclette, Camembert and Vieux Lille to the milder cheeses like Emmental. Margaret on the other hand had yet to meet a cheese here in Paris that she didn't love. The two of them were patiently working their way through all the cheeses that Monsieur Gérard carried in his shop. He was in on it now, and he wrapped George II's little morsels of cheese separately. George II could smell her coming up the stairs and would be yowling with anticipation by the time she reached the door. Most importantly, George II was someone excited to see her when she came home, even if it was partly for the treats, and he was an excellent companion to snuggle with on cold nights.

Margaret's biggest struggle in France was making friends. Friends that were human, that is. The cats loved her, but it was the people who took a little more time. She tried the same approach she had with the cats, taking small boxes of chocolates to her neighbours, but most were reserved and a bit suspicious of her. She was working on an elderly neighbour, Marie, secretly recruiting her as a friend, and she did believe she was making headway. It was a fine line between recruiting and overstepping. She learned that the French make friends at a very young age and they keep these friends their whole lives. It wasn't much different for her back home really, with Rachel and Jill. Breaking into an old friendship or trying to convince someone to have another friend was something quite challenging. But she was persistent. And George II helped. She would take him down to the basement, where the landlord always had a small continental breakfast available. There was cheese, bread and occasionally pastries. He also made fantastic coffee, bless his heart. He certainly did not have to do this, but Margaret was so grateful he did. It was a great way to get to know her neighbours without stalking them. It was a very small building and Margaret was beginning to realize how lucky she had been to purchase an apartment there. People stayed here until they died, and then usually one of their relatives moved in. Somehow, one had opened up just as she was looking and the landlord seemed to approve of her. If he had not, he would not have sold the apartment to Margaret. So each morning, Margaret took George II down to breakfast which helped her socialize tremendously. Even if she was not popular, George II was and he had a lot of friends. Everyone was anxious to give him a little nibble of their breakfast and they all got a good laugh when he took a sip of someone's coffee. He was such a French cat, something they would remark on from time to time, reminding Margaret that she was most definitely *not* such a French woman.

Nevertheless, following day after day of making a point of learning who was married to whom, who had children and learning their names and asking after them, and even daring to sit at the same table as the elderly neighbour she was recruiting as her friend, things were looking up. If not friends exactly, they now smiled when they passed her on the stairs or found her at breakfast. Some were busy with children; she certainly understood those years. And what was it that made French children the cutest children in the world? Maybe it was the French that they spoke so adorably. Or maybe it was the fact that they seemed really well behaved.

There were only thirty people in the building and she was making it her mission to win them over one by one. The kids were easy. It was the adults that were her true challenge. She knew it would not be easy and that it would take time. Americans leap into friendship and then drop them just as easily. The French, she noticed, were not interested in these 'fake' friendships. They were only interested in the real deal, the lifetime friendship. They were not going to invest their time, if they thought she was not in it for the long haul.

Well, she would have to prove it to them. She felt that the next step was to try to stuff as many neighbours as possible into her tiny apartment for wine. Surely, they would come for free wine. This would call for a trip to the *caviste*. She was happy for the excuse. She could spend hours there as it was a kind of candy store for adults. The *caviste* in her neighbourhood was one of those unusually gregarious Frenchmen and she was grateful for it. He would let her stay all afternoon and try different wines, because he was truly passionate about the wines he carried. She always bought a bottle or two, but did not need any after her afternoon spent taste testing. She inevitably left a bit tipsy. She wanted his expertise today because her neighbours would know the difference between a good wine and a subpar wine. And she would ask Monsieur Gérard for the perfect *fromage* to go with her wine. He would take his time now with her, considering the choices before him. He had maybe fifty choices of cheese on any given day. It boggled Margaret's mind. She told Monsieur Gérard that she would like to try them all and at this she was rewarded with his first smile. He utterly beamed. She fairly danced out the door.

She posted a handwritten note on the small bulletin board that hung in the lobby. Usually, people would post flyers to an art showing or requests for a good handyman. Margaret hoped she wasn't out of line, but willing to take that risk, she pinned up her little invitation, hoping at least two or three neighbours would show up.

It was summertime, which like every other season, she found to be magical in Paris. There were flowers practically bursting out of gardens and shops and people stretched picnic blankets along the Seine to take in the sunshine. They dumped sand for miles along the Seine to turn it into a beach and called it the *Paris Plage*. It was delightful. There was a lightness in the air today and Margaret had her window open and a record playing. The previous owner had left a couple belongings, and to her surprise and delight, one had been a small vintage record player and a few French records. What was it about *Les Champs-Elysées* by Joe Dassin that lifted her spirits and made her sing along? She was nervous no one would show up to her little soirée tonight, but surely at least Marie would come.

She was humming along to the music and finishing up her cheese plate when she heard a knock on the door. It was Marie, holding a lovely bouquet. Margaret was so pleased that she hugged her, something she typically reserved for close friends. Graciously, Marie embraced her back, even though the French don't hug, and began speaking all about her day and the heat and how she couldn't wait for all of the teenagers to be back in school. Margaret felt like Marie was opening up, and as they clinked their champagne glasses, there was another knock on the door. It was the young family who lived above her. They had brought pastries that their daughter was delighted to offer Margaret. More neighbours arrived, and then more. Every single person brought her something. Chocolates or flowers or little candies. Margaret thought she counted twenty-two people in the apartment at one time. She couldn't believe that many people could even fit in her apartment, let alone that that many would accept her invitation. It was the first time since moving to Paris that she thought, *I'm home*.

As the night settled down, five people remained, a couple around Margaret's age; two women in their twenties who were renting their apartment from a family friend; and Marie. The group shared stories and laughed into the evening. Finally, Marie looked at Margaret and said, "I must say, I am awfully glad you are with us. But, if you will, tell me how on earth did you get here?"

Margaret smiled as she refilled everyone's wine. It certainly wasn't a short story.

Partie Deux
L'étudiante

Greenwich, Connecticut
Twenty years earlier

Chapter 2

Margaret's heart swelled, every time she reminisced about the adventure she began, almost twenty years ago. All she had intended to do was go back to school and learn some French, thinking it was time to take a break from the corporate world while fulfilling a lifetime goal of learning a second language. She was just suffering from burnout, probably. She had assumed she'd end up taking a few years for herself, learning French, reading and walking, just a short break from the demands of work, and then she'd be back in the office. They had assured her that she could come back.

Her family thought she had utterly lost her mind when she announced she had quit her lucrative job as an attorney at a large law firm to return to college to study French. And she probably had. She was highly intelligent but was not the most mentally stable person. Her list of anxieties grew every day coupled, with several phobias and a bit of obsessive-compulsive disorder mixed in. To put it succinctly, she was a mess. She'd worked with a therapist for years, who certainly had her work cut out for her. Margaret always tried to swallow her pride and tell her everything, and her doctor was reassuring her all the time that she was normal, that she just felt more than most and was probably too smart for her own good.

"All of these worries just mean that you care deeply," she explained.

But Margaret wished she didn't care, she truly did. Why couldn't she be one of those people who just went through life carefree? She would come home after dinner with friends late at night. She might have run over a small pothole in the road along the way, but by the time she got home she was convinced it was a dog, or far worse, a person. She would have to watch the news to make sure that no one had fled the scene of a hit and run that day. And if by chance there was a report in a different city, she would have to reassure herself that, no, she was not in Boston last night.

Stability and routine were key in keeping her sane, or sane-ish, so she was not surprised when her ex-husband David was a bit unsettled when she shared her Big News. "Are you serious, babe?" he said, trying to keep his voice neutral. Would he ever stop calling her 'babe', she wondered?

"Don't get me wrong, I respect the sudden spontaneity from you, but don't you think it's a little late in life to be taking on this kind of project? I don't think you have enough time left and I think I read somewhere that our ability to learn a foreign language peaks at, like, age ten." He knew how to get her going. In fact, he knew how to light the fire under her. By questioning her ability, he knew that would just make her want it all the more. The 'enough time left' really goaded her. She was forty-five, not eighty-five. It was possible that she was getting a bit sensitive about her age these days. Her kids thought she was old. Now apparently David thought so too, even though he was two months older than her. Was she over the hill? No, she was getting into the second half of her life, and she was going to use it wisely, not just how everyone else expected her to.

Back then there were still days when Margaret questioned her decision to end their marriage. This was not one of those days.

"Well," she began, taking a deep breath in hopes of masking her frustration, "first of all, it's not spontaneous. I have been wanting to learn French since I was in middle school." *Which I told you about two hundred times*, she shouted inside her head. "Secondly, while the ability to learn to speak another language without an accent, peaks around age ten, one's ability to become fluent is largely dependent on one's intelligence and discipline. Have you ever heard Bradley Cooper speak French? He spent six months studying in Aix-en-Provence when he was at the university there and he still keeps up the language. You should hear him in interviews. He sounds so French and he can even joke in French with the interviewer. If he can do it, so can I. Or what about Serena Williams? She said she learned French because she wanted to win the French Open and when she won, she wanted to speak French when she was interviewed. She's even teaching her child French now." Margaret was on a roll.

David smiled at her and she couldn't help but smile back. She relished the brief moments when she had the upper hand intellectually. They were both extremely bright, but it had always driven her mad that David was just a little bit smarter. The fact that he never seemed to care infuriated her all the more.

In most ways, David was her polar opposite. Outgoing, laid-back and charming in the most infuriating way to someone as socially awkward as Margaret. He had smiled at her across the law library and that was it; she never stood a chance. Of course, as the story goes, it was all the things that initially attracted her to David that in the end drew them apart. His incessant tardiness and affinity for forgetting to tell her about gatherings he had committed them to until the last minute were adorable at twenty-three and utterly maddening at forty.

When Margaret confided in her friends about her painful decision to end their marriage, they all told her how sorry they were, but how happy they were that David was cooperating completely. They weren't fighting over every last possession; didn't despise each other as so many of her divorced friends did. However right they might have been, Margaret thought that perhaps it would be easier if she hated him. She could vent with her friends over chardonnay about how angry she was with him and how happy she was to be moving

on. Truth be told, she still adored David as a
was a wonderful father and loyal friend. It w
Margaret was her worst self as his wife —
flustered, irritable. She loved him but didn't love herself
when she was with him.

Her parents were upset. They did not like the idea
of divorce. People of their generation did not typically
divorce, and David was a good man. It was challenging
to explain it to them and they all three cried, but
Margaret stuck to her resolution. She wanted to be the
best person she could be, she told them, and she could
not be that person with David. In the end, they supported
her. She was petrified of losing their love, terrified of
them loving David more than her. Once, her mother had
sided with David in an argument and Margaret had
stared at her mom in disbelief. "I'm your child," she had
blubbered. "You're supposed to always side with your
child." Her parents had soothed her, telling her that their
love for her was unconditional, and she believed them.
But she would always try to please them, always try to
make them proud. She feared she was letting everyone
down by divorcing David, and yet she went ahead with
it, knowing it was something she had to do.

It was certainly an adjustment living without him.
She had gone from her parents' home, to her college
roommates, to her husband, never having lived alone.
For the first few weeks after she moved out, Margaret
awoke to every noise. She shot up in bed when she heard

the slightest of creaks, creaks that she would never have noticed before.

One particularly pitiful night, which she had never told anyone about, she hit rock bottom. A loud thunderstorm was booming outside, and she was still feeling jumpy after only two weeks on her own. Her clock told her it was two in the morning, which she always considered the 'scary time'. She figured if anyone was going to break in and murder her, it was going to happen between two and four in the morning. As she lay awake, already on edge, she was suddenly sent into a panic when her house alarm went off. In all her years of religiously setting the alarm, she'd never actually had one go off while she was home.

Naturally, she assumed that someone was in her house. She was literally shaking as she called the police, hiding in her closet. In a complete panic, she then raced to the front door, not caring that she was sleeping in one of David's old white t-shirts. It came almost to her knees, but all she had on underneath was an old pair of panties. The police officer stood dripping in the pouring rain when she opened the door. He was kind, clearly feeling sympathetic towards her, and told her he would walk the perimeter to see if there were any signs of break-in, though he was confident it was just the storm that had set off the alarm. He came back drenched, assuring her that all windows and doors were locked and secure. She so wanted him to search inside. Did he not realize that the murderer was surely hiding in the house?

But, standing there huddled on the front porch, she became aware of her state of undress and wasn't sure she really wanted to subject herself, or this poor man, to any more embarrassment. She thanked him and closed the door, feeling not the slightest bit calmer.

She stood there in the hallway, heart still beating fast and not thinking rationally. It only took her a second to spot the keys on the table by the door. She grabbed them, ran out to the car parked in the driveway and jumped in. She couldn't go to a hotel. She was not dressed and she did not have her purse. She'd look like an insane person. But at this point, her irrational terror had taken over and there was no chance she was entering the house again tonight. She could sleep here in the car, she thought. It was only a few hours until morning. Surely the intruder would take what he wanted and leave. She tilted the seat back, but it would not lay flat.

She was squirming around trying to get comfortable when along came the nightly neighbourhood watch, circling the block and being far too diligent in his job. It would be humiliating if he saw her in her car and of course he would stop and ask her why she was there, so she ducked as he came by. It was hot in the car and she had to crack the windows to let in a little air. She couldn't open them much because of the bad guy and because it was raining pretty hard. Around came the guard not ten minutes later, and she ducked again. She realized the next time that he circled that she could not spend the entire night watching for the guard and ducking. She would sleep in the back of the car, doors locked. She dashed around the car, opened the back of her SUV and jumped in quickly. She was pretty wet and sticky, but safe. There was enough room for her to lay down in a half moon position and she actually felt that when her heartbeat slowed down, maybe she would be able to fall asleep. But it was terribly uncomfortable and it didn't take her long to remember that weeks before David had left, he had borrowed her car to bring home some sod. So she was sleeping on bits of grass and dirt.

That was it. She was exhausted, it was now three-thirty in the morning and she no longer cared what happened to her. Well, she cared a little. She slept on the sofa in the living room, all the lights on, with her phone in her hand. But she was able to get a couple hours sleep. That was actually a turning point. From then on, she usually could sleep through the night. It was as if she had to go through this humiliating episode to realize she could do this.

So here she was — forty-five, single and embarking on this strange but exciting new journey. She was nervous, perhaps even scared, but so certain that this was the right path. Her parents had unexpectedly embraced her decision. Their support was so important to her. She would always go to great lengths to make them proud of her. They would have been up in arms just ten years ago if she had quit. But when she explained that learning French was bringing her back to life, making her feel alive, they agreed it was time for a change.

Every French word she learned, she relished. The French language was just so incredibly beautiful. Margaret once read that there was a committee in France, the *Académie Française*, for matters pertaining to the French language. There were forty members on the committee, and new members were elected by the committee itself. Members were known as *les immortels*, as they remained for life, studying each new word to see if it merited being added to the French language. To get onto this committee was akin to getting a seat on a rocket to Mars. Many famous writers such as Jules Verne, Sartre, Baudelaire and Proust were all denied membership. The whole concept was mind-blowing, but they must have been doing something right because how could you beat the beauty of a word such as *arc-en-ciel* (rainbow) or *âme-sœur* (soulmate — which literally translates as soul sister)? She could go on and on. Each word was her new favourite.

Perfectionist that she was, Margaret was studying before she had even started school, which was just weeks away. She had bought the textbook which had been so exciting. She was pretty sure the university bookstore employee was thinking that this helicopter mom was buying books for her child, but she was not explaining herself today. Notebooks had been purchased at Target with all the mothers and their children heading back to elementary school, with dividers of course, and pockets in the dividers for anything the teacher might hand out, index cards for flash cards, which she had already written on and gone through. She already needed more — the vocabulary was endless. She also bought yellow sticky notes and covered every object in her house in them. *Le lit* was stuck to her bed and *les livres* to her books, *l'étagère* on her bookshelf and *la bougie* on the candle. If she could stick a note onto *la fourmi* (the ant) she saw on the floor, she would.

She was listening to the podcast *Coffee Break French* for ten or fifteen minutes a day and trying *Slow News French*, which was a bit beyond her grasp.

Margaret was a bit concerned about what to wear to school. Should she go back to school shopping? That was her favourite thing when she was a kid. It seemed like a good idea to change her wardrobe as she changed her whole life. Anyway, she certainly couldn't wear suits and business dresses to school. But that was all she owned. Sifting through her closet, she realized she hated her clothes. She went to the kitchen, got several big black plastic bags. Maybe someone somewhere was going through a life change like she was, but going in the opposite direction and now needed new work clothes. She would donate them. She started stuffing clothes into the bags, and quickly realized that everything needed to come out for her to really purge. Very Marie Kondo. She had read *The Life-Changing*

Magic of Tidying Up once and then promptly placed it on her bookshelf and forgot all about it — until now. She would only choose what 'sparked joy'. When all was said and done, she only had one pair of jeans and a couple t-shirts that she realized she really loved. There was one cashmere grey sweater as well and her favourite pair of sneakers. That was it. She hung up her jeans and put the t-shirts in the dresser, rolling them up as Marie had instructed in her very helpful book.

Now what? Where did someone her age shop? She had always had a personal shopper when she was a lawyer. She was too busy and her salary allowed her to have that luxury. Well, that was a thing of the past. She would be on a budget from now on. She had enough to keep her going for maybe five years on the lifestyle she was accustomed to, but to sustain her for longer with no income, or very little income, a budget was a must. Well, said budget was going to have to wait until she had done a little shopping.

She actually hated shopping, hence why she had paid someone to do it. She didn't have one of those perfect bodies where even clothes from a garage sale look good. Her body was just fine — good, but not great. She was tall, almost five foot eight inches. Not thin, but not overweight. Her breasts were small, and no matter how much she sucked it in, she always had a little tummy pooch. Being a perfectionist, this was hard to take in the glaring dressing room lights. But now she was determined to give up trying to be so perfect. It never seemed to work anyway. She was going to have fun shopping and be grateful for the body she was given.

Now, where to go. She texted Claire. *S.O.S. Where do people shop?!* Claire, her beautiful daughter, tall and fair like her, but slender and with an actual figure, was at NYU in her sophomore year, studying linguistics. The apple did not fall far from the tree. She was a bit jealous of Claire, just beginning life, the whole world at her feet. She had truly gotten all of Margaret's best traits and none of her worst. She was brave, confident, smart and beautiful.

She knew that people found her, Margaret, endearing because of, or maybe it was in spite of, all her quirks. David had said that he had fallen in love with her because she was independent yet vulnerable. She had loved that and never forgotten it, but oh to be brave and confident. Claire had no idea what she possessed. Of course, you do not realize it when you are twenty, but with all the options out there, it was an exciting time for her whether she realized it or not. Actually, so many changes happen in your twenties. You go to school possibly, you might get your first job, your first house, you might meet the person you want to marry or spend your life with, you could even have a child. Phew, that's a lot in one decade.

Margaret took a moment to say a prayer that Claire made wise decisions. It was a joke with them. As a teenager, every time Claire left the house, Margaret would say, "Make wise decisions."

And Claire would say, "Sure, Mom".

Once when she was home from college, she laughed with Margaret about the fact that her mom telling her to make wise decisions did not really ensure that she would indeed make wise decisions. But it had to be said, Margaret countered.

Of course, she said the same to her son Joseph. Sweet Joseph, so like his father. He was tall, like the rest of the family, with darker hair than the rest of them. He was handsome, but he didn't know it, even though he got a lot of attention from girls. She didn't worry as much with Joseph. He was more of a serious kid, typical first child, very type A, very ambitious. But still, he was a teenager and she worried. One time, he had a bunch of friends up in his room. She felt it was time to check on them and went upstairs, gave a quick knock on the door, and opened it. Or tried to. The sofa in his room had been pulled against the door so no one could open it. She tried to keep her voice even as she told Joseph to please open the door. She could hear the scurrying and muffled voices and it was so obvious they were hiding something. They were seniors in high school. What did she expect? It never even crossed her mind it might be drugs, and thankfully it wasn't, but she could smell the alcohol as soon as she entered the room. And the guilty faces confirmed her suspicions. She had everyone give her their keys, had them spend the night and sent them home the next morning.

She and Joseph had a good talk that morning about wise decisions and he listened, but she hoped he heard. She also told him that this was a G-rated house, and there would never be alcohol on the premises again as long as they were under-age. Inside she was thinking, please let this be as serious as it ever gets.

Joseph had been her buddy as a little boy. They used to hold hands as they drove around town, and they had mother-son date nights on Friday. She adored Joseph with all her heart. She knew that he sometimes was jealous of all the time she spent with Claire, and it worried her so much that it hurt his feelings. It was just that Claire was so into the same things as she was, and as she grew up, they turned into friends who happened to have very similar interests. They could talk all day. David sometimes said that she and Claire made him dizzy. He could only take the two of them in small chunks. She knew that this close of a relationship with a son was rare and perhaps not even healthy. He needed to break away, as painful as it was. But Joseph was her rock. She could always count on him; she knew he would always be there for her as she would for him. And she loved both her children equally and ferociously.

While trying to tamp down parental guilt, she saw that Claire had sent her several names of Instagram accounts of people in cute clothes. Margaret hated social media, and was reluctant to admit how quickly she got sucked in. Hours later, her shoulders hurt and she regretted wasting so much time, but she had found several clothing companies that interested her. Faherty, with a focus on sustainable clothing intrigued her. She bought a pair of rolled up khaki pants and a couple shirts. She also liked Amour Vert (maybe the French name caught her eye). She loved how many of the clothes were recycled and the tennis shoes she bought were made from rubber instead of leather. She probably didn't need another pair of tennis shoes, considering they were now the only type of shoe that she *did* have, but she was committed to purchasing what she liked, not what she thought she should like. She splurged on a couple other basics from some high-end, sustainable brands, and ended with her new favourite, Antik Batik. Of course it was French, and the clothing was just her style, or at least just what she would like to be her style. Slightly bohemian but feminine. Blouses that could be tucked in or left untucked. Gorgeous dresses that could be worn day or night. She completed her shopping with a couple pairs of sandals, gulped at the money she had spent, and decided that clothing purchases were officially done.

When the clothes came in, it felt like Christmas. She loved each unique piece and hung them carefully in the closet on wood hangers purchased from Target. There wasn't much in her closet but it was actually liberating. This was a capsule wardrobe, she realized, and she instantly embraced it. She felt lighter. It would be easy to choose clothes each day because there were not many choices. She had two pairs of jeans, two pairs of pants, one skirt, two dresses and five blouses. A few new t-shirts were in her dresser and she had kept a couple blazers that she could layer over these. Her closet looked amazing. Clean. The opposite of stress. She lay down on the floor and felt the freedom of owning only what she loved. Plus, she thought enthusiastically, it was very French. The French prided themselves on having very few clothes, but they were all quality pieces. They might only own two sweaters but they would be high quality cashmere. That may have come about because they had only tiny places to store their clothes, but it really worked for them. The French were always beautifully dressed. They went for quality over quantity, and were not embarrassed to wear the same pair of pants several times a week, or a shirt either. They just tossed on a scarf to change the outfit. Surely, she had some silk scarfs in a drawer somewhere that she used to wear.

She brought in her daughter to confirm that her purchases were okay. Claire seemed impressed, even finding a few things she wanted to borrow, which Margaret took as an excellent sign that she had chosen well. Claire even said that she was inspired to try a capsule wardrobe herself. Margaret beamed. It inspired her to 'Marie Kondo' other parts of her house. Why in the world did she have things on coffee tables and in bookshelves that she did not love?

Before she knew it, she had reached the night before the big day. She lay out her cutest outfit; a simple tee with a blazer, cropped jeans and her new tennis shoes. Singing along to *Soulman* by Ben l'Oncle Soul, she got herself ready for bed. She hopped under the covers and started binge watching old Julia Child cooking shows. Was there anything more soothing than listening to Julia Child's distinctive voice reassuring us all that we could, indeed, make duck paté with goose fat. Never mind the question of where does one begin to dream of getting goose fat. Julia Child was such an inspiration to Margaret. What an independent strong woman, working during World War II for the government in Sri Lanka. She was a very tall woman for the 1920s, but at six foot two, she carried herself confidently. Margaret sometimes rounded her shoulders to make herself shorter and she was only five foot eight. Lucky Julia, she met a man who worked in Paris, so off she went to the Cordon Bleu to become the famous author of *Mastering the Art of French Cooking*.

Margaret fell asleep dreaming of boeuf bourguignon and the new life that lay ahead.

Chapter 3

Margaret walked into the classroom and took a deep breath. The language building was certainly nothing to brag about. It was dingy and dimly lit. Maybe it was dimly lit because it was dingy. She imagined it hadn't been updated since she herself was a college student; it was far too warm and when she inhaled her nose was filled with dust and old books. Truthfully, she loved that smell. It reminded her of studying in the most hidden corners of the library in law school. While the other students preferred burning the midnight oil, she loved to go there at the crack of dawn; thermos of coffee in one hand, freshly sharpened pencil in the other, with nothing but a big stack of books to keep her company.

Her train of thought was interrupted as two young students walked into the classroom noisily chattering. The girls' outfits were identical, short athletic shorts, oversized t-shirts and sloppy ponytails. Margaret immediately felt foolish in her blazer. When she was a college student everyone dressed nicely. But, still, she liked her clothes. *These spark joy*, she reminded herself. Plus, she was in her forties, she was not nineteen. She would have felt silly trying to dress like a teenager.

"Excuse me, hi! Are you the professor?" the taller girl inquired cheerfully.

Margaret was baffled. She had wedged herself into one of the way-too-small desks with her notepad and textbook stacked neatly next to her blue pen and highlighter. Did they think she was one of those hip professors who sat in the same seats as the students to be 'one with the class' or something? Or was it just because she was old?

Before she could answer her own question, in strolled a beautiful young woman with cropped hair, wearing a casual sundress and a chic little backpack. "Salut," she said warmly.

"Oh, uh, sorry," the girl stammered, awkwardly backing away from Margaret.

So this is the professor, she thought. *Great. Not only am I clearly the oldest student, I am also older than the teacher.*

Fortunately, her professor seemed unfazed by this fact, and introduced herself as Madame Hansen. She was cheerful, but spoke in a laid-back tone. When she took her oversized sunglasses off her head, Margaret noticed that she had a purple streak in her short brown hair.

"*Bonjour. Je m'appelle Madame Hansen. Comment vous appelez-vous?*"

The other students looked frozen in fear, but Margaret's heart was racing with excitement.

49

Oh, I know the answer! she thought excitedly. Of course, she had already studied the first chapter. In fact, she had memorized it.

Hating to be the old lady *and* the teacher's pet, she gave the other students a minute to respond. However, when no one volunteered, she couldn't help herself. She looked around smiling, and began to slowly raise her hand.

"Bonjour, Madame Hansen. Je m'appelle Margaret."

"Très bien, Margaret," Madame Hansen said, smiling kindly. The tall girl sitting next to her gave her a thumbs up.

Margaret listened intently while the professor explained to the class that *je m'appelle* translates to 'I call myself' or 'my name is', encouraging the rest of the class to introduce themselves.

Madame Hansen patiently listened to each shaky introduction, responding to each student with phrases such as *bien fait* or *enchantée*.

Margaret could tell immediately that she was going to like Madame Hansen, something she was grateful for considering she was one of only two French professors at the small university. If Margaret was really going to see this dream through, they would be spending quite a bit of time together.

She knew her accent was atrocious, but Margaret was certain that, with enough work, she could ace every test. She actually studied, and may well have been the only one in class who did. She had yellow sticky notes stuck to every surface in her house. She had added more since her first school shopping purchases and now *la commode* was glued to her dresser and *le bureau* to her desk. There must have been over a hundred sticky notes. Even George got a new collar that read 'George le chat', George the cat. So much for the peaceful Marie Kondo look she had been going for. Claire and Joseph joked that they could learn French just by spending time in her house. She laughed watching the movie Julie and Julia, as Julia tried to learn French. But she persevered and it had paid off. She had become fluent and Margaret, stubborn as she was, would not give up until she could carry on conversations with little effort.

One week in, they had their first quiz. Margaret prepped for it as if it were the bar exam. To be fair, it wasn't like she had much else going on. But it was more than that; she desperately wanted to succeed. And she enjoyed studying. And unlike her previous academic endeavours, she actually wanted this for herself.

The next day, Madame Hansen returned the graded quizzes. Margaret was impressed with the quick turnaround. Beginning to pass out the papers, Madame Hansen called out in a sing-song voice "someone made a hundred!" Margaret's face turned beet red, knowing that everyone knew who that someone was.

"Good job!" Margaret looked over to see the girl who had mistaken her for the professor smiling genuinely.

She tried to shrug the compliment off. Kids seemed nicer these days. Parents must be doing something right. "Beginner's luck," she said casually. Inside she was jumping up and down. And of course, she called her mom, the only one who was excited over the smallest achievements. Characteristically, she raved about Margaret's tiny success and Margaret knew she would be calling her friends to tell them about it.

She didn't care that there was no point to learning French; she didn't really care if she even got her degree. She just loved it. What a breath of fresh air it was to work hard at something, not because she was expected to or because she felt she had something to prove, but simply because it pleased her. Everyone tried to talk her into taking Spanish. She got the usual 'it's so much more practical' speeches, but she would not be swayed. She knew what she wanted, for once in her life.

She had visited Claire in Spain when Claire spent the summer in Valencia after her freshman year, 'studying Spanish'. So she and her friends said. Margaret arrived in Barcelona and took the one-hour train down to Valencia. Claire and her friends were there to greet her at the train station, which she so appreciated, but one look at Claire and she knew she was hungover. She knew her daughter. After a giant hug, thank goodness she still got those, Claire darted to the bathroom. She tried to play it off as just a late night and some bad food, but Claire was not a total angel. Margaret found out the disco they went to — yes, they still had discos in Spain — opened at midnight. They had stayed until five a.m. And yes, drinking had been involved. Had they been doing this all summer?

Margaret took deep breaths. She had just watched the movie *Taken*, against the advice of David. She could not hold back. "Claire," she admonished. "If you are not in control, someone could so easily take advantage of you, or literally take you." Margaret had tears in her eyes. This child was her joy. Claire could see how distraught she was and reassured her that the four friends she lived with looked out for each other. Margaret gave her the please, please make wise decisions speech for the umpteenth time and prayed that God would protect this precious girl.

She found out Spanish was not for her. She loved the culture. Spanish people were so friendly and warm. She loved the food. Yes, to paella and sangria. The beauty of the country could not be denied. It was stunning, as was the architecture. Gaudi's Sagrada Familia in Barcelona left her gaping in wonder. But, the French language in her opinion was more beautiful. Paris was where her heart was and there were issues with Spain — for one thing, the Spaniards didn't eat dinner until nine. That was her bedtime. The restaurants were quite simply not open until nine p.m. Everyone was home taking a siesta because they had been partying all night. This was a vicious cycle. They didn't start their work day until ten in the morning. This was shocking to Margaret who was never at the office later than seven a.m. And lunch was not served in Spain until three. She was hungry the entire time she was in Spain.

No, she would take the civilized French any day. They might drink gallons of wine, but they had themselves home at a decent hour and you could eat any time you wanted. The boulangeries and the patisseries were open at all times. No one was home taking a three-hour nap, for goodness sake. And the bread. Only the French knew how to do bread. No preservatives, hard as a rock in three hours, it had to be eaten right away. That was the way to do it. Hot out of the oven with some butter. Most of all, the patisseries. The pain au chocolat and the macarons. Oh, and of course, even though the architecture in Spain was outstanding, she herself preferred the buildings and streets in France. She was so grateful it had not been totally destroyed in World War II. She had been told that the Germans felt they could not destroy something so beautiful. They had made a wise decision.

She loved learning French the way someone else might love to cook or play golf. Her anxieties were quickly forgotten when she studied the language. She got into what her yoga magazines called 'the flow', meaning she was so involved in what she was doing, that no other thoughts entered her mind. She forgot that she might be dying or that she may have left the oven on. She had struggled with anxiety all her life, having tried acupuncture, chamomile tea, hypnosis, therapy and even at times medication. But when she studied

French, she felt calm. All the would-haves, should-haves, might-haves drifted away, replaced with beautiful words like *papillon* and *fleur*. She wanted to collect these words and wrap them around her to keep her safe.

Margaret wondered how she could possibly describe such a profound feeling. Who in her life would understand how their neurotic yet logical friend was now spending her days pouring over the words of Proust and Baudelaire? The thought of explaining to her book club girlfriends (who had not actually read, or even chosen, a book in nine years) that she was finally fulfilling her life's dream made her squirm. She had lovely friends; it was just that she had never really shown them her whole self. She wasn't even sure she had shown it to her family. In fact, she was beginning to realize that it wasn't until now that she was discovering who she was deep down.

She had spent a lifetime pleasing others. In a way, pleasing others made her happy, but it was not right and could not make her feel completely content because it was like chasing after an unattainable dream. It was impossible, which probably fuelled her anxiety. She would never, ever make everyone happy and she needed to stop trying. She fully understood the mid-life crisis now. That crossroads of there is only so much time left and how do I want to spend it. But this didn't feel like a crisis; this felt like something positive, something good. She was making a major change and she was aware that others saw this as a mid-life crisis, but she didn't agree. She felt like she had just woken up and realized that she and she alone had the choice to make the life she wanted. Not to live the life others wanted for her. How could she not have realized this earlier? She had always held the power to make her own decisions and yet she had let others do it for her. That stopped now. She was incredibly thankful that she had finally become aware that her life was hers.

Rather than further freak out her loved ones with tales of her spiritual awakening, Margaret instead, gave the same line every time someone asked her what on earth she was doing going back to school to learn French. "Oh, you know, I've always wanted to travel, and France is first on my bucket list. I figure it would be smart to learn the language."

"Ah, yes," they would all smile, comforted to hear that their overachieving, under-adventurous friend had not left them entirely, "you are always prepared for everything, aren't you!"

"You know me," she would say warmly, knowing full well that no one expected her to take that trip. Nonetheless, everyone was satisfied with the answer; a clear, concise reason for her sudden life change. God forbid, she do something just for pleasure. That would be very un-Margaret.

While it was a line to keep people from prying, the truth was that Margaret did desperately dream of traveling again. She wanted to stretch herself beyond her fear and into the courage she knew she possessed. She wanted to inhale the intoxicating scent of *la lavande* in Provence; to dip her toes into the blue waters off of the Côte d'Azur. She wanted to practice her French with the locals; to go to a quiet little bistro each morning and order *un café crème et un croissant, s'il vous plaît*. She wanted to wander through cosy bookstores and re-read her favourite novels in French in the Jardin du Luxembourg. Just daydreaming about it set her mind at ease and steadied her heartbeat. The desire was slowly trumping the fear and winning.

'Travel to France alone' had been at the top of her list of goals for years. She loved taking trips with her friends and family, but she dreamed of exploring this magical country all by herself. She wanted to add Live in France' to her list, but at the time it seemed too much to ask. She kept the running list on her phone, something she began after her divorce as a way to get inspired for the future. In her mind, spending a few weeks in France was the ultimate dream. She wanted to go all by herself and soak up every morsel of culture and food like a sponge. When she asked herself, *what is it I want most*, she didn't respond as most people did with answers like, 'travel the world' or 'live on a sailboat for a year'. Instantly and easily, she knew her big, secret dream was to live in France.

She imagined herself living in a little apartment above a boulangerie where she could spend her days practicing French and eating bread guilt-free. She would walk for miles so she could eat even more bread and perhaps it would even out so she wouldn't get too pudgy. If not, she wouldn't care. It would be difficult to be far from family and friends, but they would visit. She would take them to Provence and the Côte d'Azur and to the Loire Valley and oh, they would have to go to Burgundy too! While she loved to indulge in this daydream, she couldn't imagine it becoming a reality. So a solo-trip to France would have to suffice. She saw it each time she opened her list and felt a little jolt of excitement as she considered booking her adventure.

Until, of course, she thought about the fact that she would have to step foot on an airplane to get there.

Chapter 4

While everyone was too polite to acknowledge it, they all knew that it was 'the incident' last year that would keep her from flying. The incident was not something that Margaret ruminated on fondly, considering it involved her having a minor panic attack aboard a plane, almost causing an emergency landing. She and her two closest friends had planned a girls' trip to Maine. They were going to eat fresh lobster rolls and sip crisp Sauvignon Blanc by the sea. The girls loved traveling together; this sacred time was good for the soul in the midst of busy careers, relationship ups and downs and children to care for. But life being hectic as it was, it had been two years since their last getaway.

It had not just been two years since her last girl's getaway, but since Margaret had taken any trip further than just a weekend to the city with Claire. This meant, of course, that it had been two years since she had flown on an airplane.

This time, the panic she felt rising in her chest could not be squandered, and before she knew it, she found herself breathing into an airsickness bag while a flight attendant checked her pulse. As the plane landed, Margaret mentally banished air-travel for the foreseeable future. The girls all took the train home in solidarity, never once teasing Margaret, all knowing in their own way what it feels like to experience paralyzing fear.

Margaret would quite honestly have avoided flying her whole life if it weren't for her deep love of travel and her strong fear of missing out. "It's called FOMO, Mom, and you have it bad," Claire had once told her.

So, due to her FOMO and her, perhaps valid, fear of turning into a recluse, Margaret stepped aboard flight after flight and never regretted it, no matter how much the nervousness turned her stomach. Along with the occasional family vacation, she and Claire had been fortunate enough to travel to some extraordinary places. Every year they gave each other the same gift for Christmas, a mother-daughter trip that they would then take that summer. At the same time, David would take Joseph fly-fishing or climbing somewhere exotic. The sort of activities that scared Margaret to death.

She was rather proud of herself for traveling so often, seeing as she was deeply afraid to fly. She would start getting nervous several days before the trip, hoping that maybe she would get sick or a work emergency would come up so she wouldn't have to go. Once she made it, the process would be repeated when it came to flying home. But always, the trips were worth it. She and Claire had been to Florence, Venice and Rome. They had taken a Mediterranean cruise going all the way to Croatia. Margaret visited Claire in Valencia when she spent six weeks studying in Spain in high school. They had travelled to Lucerne in Switzerland and Santorini in Greece.

Although Margaret was the most organized person she knew, she often had common sense lapses, particularly when she was feeling anxious or flustered. So when she was in charge of escorting her daughter around foreign countries, things did not always go smoothly. Once, they had gotten lost in Florence and had completely forgotten the name of their hotel. Claire was irate that her mother hadn't thought to write it down. Things got a bit dicey when they had trouble finding someone who spoke English well enough to help them out. They were hot, hungry and jet-lagged, and to their utter embarrassment, they eventually had to ask a very grouchy police officer for assistance. Claire was grumpy and mad at her for getting them lost but forgave her quickly. Margaret had a terrible sense of direction and found herself lost all the time, so these instances were not unexpected.

On another trip, distracted by the chocolate shop at the station, they had completely missed their train in Switzerland, leaving them stuck in a tiny town with no hotel. Margaret didn't want to take her daughter wandering around in the night, so they wound up staying overnight at the train station on hard benches. Margaret stayed awake the whole night, guarding her sleeping daughter with pepper spray she carried on her keychain.

The worst travel mistake Margaret had made was allowing them to miss their cruise ship while visiting a tiny island in Greece. The trip was Claire's graduation present; she had always dreamt of having a '*Mamma Mia* moment' in Greece. They made the mistake of consulting their guide book rather than the actual cruise ship guide. They spotted the most beautiful beach that they just *had* to go to, despite knowing nothing about the island. The book used phrases like 'off the beaten path' and 'rustic local spot', which should have been red flags. Margaret thought it sounded great — less crowded and stressful than all of the touristy beaches — so they jumped in a cab and off they went. The beach was fairly deserted and there were no amenities; no bathrooms, no restaurants. They tried to banish their gut feeling that they were making a mistake. It was, in their defence, the most pristine water they had ever seen. Set in a cove, with rocky mountains behind them, and the warm crystal clear water in front of them, they leaped into the water, put on their snorkelling gear and got lost in time looking at all the colourful fish.

Sometime later, Margaret realized that they better head back to the boat. It had taken thirty minutes to get here after all. It didn't seem like much of a problem — the boat wasn't set to leave for a couple hours. So, they walked up to the road, sopping wet and exhausted, to hail a taxi. It quickly became clear there were no taxis. In fact, there were no cars driving by at all. The road was as quiet as could be.

Fear started to course through Margaret. Being lost in the middle of Florence was one thing. Help could be found. And snacks. She tried to stay calm for Claire, walking back down the hill to the beach to find someone who spoke English. No one did, and worse, no one seemed interested in helping them. Why did she not ask their taxi driver to return for them at a specified hour? Why did she never think of the obvious solution until it was too late? The two of them stood staring down the two-lane road. She would absolutely not let them hitchhike. Claire was too young and pretty — someone would probably kidnap her and dump Margaret. After almost thirty minutes, the panic started to rise in her and she was having trouble hiding it from Claire, who was adding to it by asking every few minutes "Mooooom, what are we going to do?" She did not want to be the adult right now. There really wasn't a good answer. She could remember which way they had come from, but not how far away the town was. But they couldn't just stay here, so they started walking.

Claire started complaining about being hot, and then she was thirsty. Margaret felt like a terrible mother. They walked and walked as Margaret frantically checked her watch. Thirty minutes until the boat left. Panic had long ago turned into sheer terror. Margaret always wished she were one of those people that let mistakes like this roll off her back. "Oh well," she tried to convince herself as much as Claire. "It's an adventure. We'll spend a night or two here. Catch a plane or a ferry later to catch up with the boat." Claire shot her a sarcastic look. She had stopped complaining but Margaret could see she was miserable. It was obvious that they could not walk all the way to the dock. They were exhausted and there was no time.

Just as she was at the point of crying, a bus slowed to a stop, tooted its horn and opened the doors. They had no idea what the driver was saying but he was ushering them into the bus and they hopped on gratefully. There was nowhere to sit, and other passengers were already standing. As well as being stuffed with people, there was also every kind of animal imaginable on board. Birds were squawking and goats were baa-ing. There were chickens sitting on several laps. People were openly staring at them, but no one smiled. The smell was atrocious but all the windows were open, letting in a sea breeze.

Despite the bizarre circumstances, Margaret began to feel some relief. She did not care about the conditions they were in, so long as they were safe and headed the right way. At least the bus was going in the right direction. As she saw the dock coming into view, she began shouting and waving her arms for the driver to stop. He got the idea and pulled up to the curb. They ran around looking for their boat, which was very obviously gone. They looked out at the ocean and could just barely make out a big white boat in the distance.

Claire raised her eyebrows at Margaret. They immediately got to work finding a local who would perhaps be willing to take them out to the boat, which was no small chore. But Claire was scrappy, and she hounded a small shop owner who admitted to having a boat until he agreed to ferry them out. As they approached the boat, their captain began explaining to them in broken English that they would have to jump from the little boat onto the cruise ship. Margaret was shocked, though she didn't know what she was expecting. Both boats were bobbing up and down in the rolling waves as a crew member from the ship opened a small door towards the bottom of the boat. The local then grabbed Claire by her lifejacket and quite literally threw her across three feet of water to the crew member aboard the ship.

"Your turn, ma'am," he shouted across the roar of the ocean. Margaret began to feel sick. She was heavier than Claire — what if the small sailor didn't have it in him to fling her all the way across? Would she drown, leaving Claire to fend for herself? Looking around in a panic, she knew she didn't have any other options. She squeezed her eyes shut as the man hoisted her up by her lifejacket and tossed her aboard. She landed with a thump, and by the time she opened her eyes again their local saviour was already tugging his way back to land.

Margaret and Claire both stood there in disbelief. "What just happened?" Claire asked, letting out a combined sigh/laugh.

As she tried to regain her composure, Margaret's stomach suddenly dropped again. "Oh my god, I didn't even pay him," she said, horrified that she hadn't thought of this initially.

"It's okay", the crew man casually told them. "Happens all the time. You were lucky we were still close by." With that, he led them up a small staircase which landed them back among the other passengers as if nothing had happened. They walked quietly back to their room and both collapsed on their beds.

Later that evening, as they ate their room service pizza, they laughed at the countless missteps they had taken that day. A remote beach, a strange animal bus and a possible-drowning, all in a matter of hours. Margaret had inadvertently broken so many of her own rules that day — strangers, germs, dangerous behaviour! Joseph would have been so mad at them. They made a pact to keep this story between them.

Claire loved reliving all of their blunders. "Remember that one time we got to the train station and you *forgot* the tickets?"

Yes, Margaret remembered it all too well. Claire would laugh about how they had to repurchase tickets for twice the original price, seemingly forgetting how grumpy she'd been at the time. Margaret hated that she lacked common sense. She hated that her anxiety and overthinking did not lead to perfectly planned-out experiences. She was a perfectionist who couldn't seem to do anything perfectly. But as she got older, she tried to give herself some credit. They survived, and the memories they made were invaluable.

Though she'd visited some wonderful places with Claire, their family and her girlfriends, France was her absolute favourite. She'd visited three times, and each time it felt like coming home. She loved everything about the country. Paris in particular was her dream city. It was the kind of city that she might actually get lost in on purpose. Even Claire didn't mind — there was always a bakery they could pop into.

Once, when Claire was fifteen, the two of them had meant to take a two-week trip traveling around Europe, starting in Paris. Margaret went through her usual pre-trip routine, panic, try to cancel, go anyway knowing she'd be glad she did. It was their first time to the city and they were completely enchanted. Once they arrived, they immediately cancelled the rest of the trip, choosing to instead stay in Paris the whole time. It was perhaps an irresponsible decision, considering they had nowhere to stay. Their hotel had kicked them out after the three days they had initially booked, as the French Open was taking place and the hotel was completely full. They walked the streets of Paris pulling their suitcases behind them, looking for literally anywhere that would take them.

Margaret did not enjoy the unknown, but in Paris, she felt a strange sense of ease she might not have felt elsewhere. Even though the streets were bumpy and the suitcases unwieldy, they were chatting and laughing. After knocking on the doors of numerous little bed and breakfasts, they finally found a room available in the

Latin Quarter. It was utterly charming, and though it was no five-star hotel, they liked it better than their previous fancy hotel in the first arrondissement. The *propriétaire* looked them over and decided they were worthy of her establishment. They could only go up the elevator one at a time. Margaret could barely stuff Claire and her suitcase in at the same time. "I'll just meet you upstairs," she yelled through the iron bars to her daughter. Claire laughed, knowing so well that her mom would be paralyzed with fear by this *petit ascenseur.* Margaret hated being enclosed in small spaces and she held her breath the entirety of the ride, praying it didn't get stuck.

Spending two weeks in the city, they could almost pretend they were residents. They quickly found favourite streets. *Rue Cler* was such fun because they discovered they could go from store to store to collect their meal. They would visit the *boulangerie* for their bread, the *boucherie* for their slices of ham and the *fromagerie* for the cheese — oh, the cheese. France professed to have over five hundred different kinds of cheese and what a joy it would be to try them all. They could then go on to the *pâtisserie* for their dessert — perhaps a macaron — and then on to the *caviste* for a bottle of wine. Margaret let Claire have a small glass with her each evening, something she never would have allowed back home. They would take their ingredients to the closest park and have a feast, plopping right down on the plush grass. Their favourite was the Jardin des

Tuileries, right next to the Louvre. They could watch children sailing little boats in the ponds and old men sitting in the famous green chairs playing dominoes. Many people were simply taking a walk or standing in line at the vendor selling *croque monsieurs* and *croque madames*.

These were some of the happiest times of her life. She basked in the sun, not caring if she added wrinkles and age spots, just content. These were also some of the only times, if she was being honest, that she was completely at peace. There was no stress, nothing to hurry to or worry about. Her headaches vanished and her body wasn't tensed up like usual. The Xanax back in the hotel room remained unopened. She took Claire everywhere, to all the museums and exhibitions, but if they felt like seeing only one or two paintings and then leaving in favour of a pastry break, they were both okay with that.

She and Claire were ideal travel partners because they enjoyed the same things. They liked to explore, but not in an overly-adventurous way. The exploring they enjoyed involved walking out of their hotel and ending up in a new neighbourhood to experience. The Marais was one of their favourites. They loved weaving in and out of the narrow and winding streets and finding a new shop or café. They had bought Claire some darling dresses in a little boutique and she looked so French, thought Margaret. In fact, Claire still revelled in the fact that someone had asked her for directions.

They made it a game to try to find the most beautiful street in the city. Every street was so unique, with its own charm. Paris is comprised of twenty neighbourhoods called *arrondissements*, they learned, and within these *arrondissements* are another eighty smaller neighbourhoods, called *quartiers*. Their goal was to visit each *arrondissement* and though they didn't even come close, they loved what they had seen. One day they accidentally discovered the covered promenades. Way back when, they had covered tiny alleyways filled with shops and restaurants so that people could get out, even in the rain and the cold. Margaret rejoiced in the fact that they still existed today, going strong.

She and Claire also loved to people-watch and dreamed of making a French friend, although they were never successful. Of the two of them, Claire was the more outgoing one, and that still wasn't saying much. However, their timidity didn't keep them from saying "Salut!" to everyone that would listen.

They always agreed that carrying-on their suitcase was the way to go. They would usually travel in May or June, so it was easy to pack dresses that they could just roll up. People were always amazed that they could fit weeks' worth of clothing into a carry-on and never wear the same thing twice. Claire packed perfectly curated little outfits while half of Margaret's suitcase was made up of energy bars and other snack foods. She had always had a crazy phobia of being hungry. That was probably fear number 231 on her never-ending list of fears. There was always a new one popping up (shoelaces caught in an escalator! Lead poisoning!), and none of the old ones ever went away. She couldn't keep track of everything that worried her.

She also had to pack plenty of wet wipes, which she used to scrub the entire interior of the airplane and hotel room. She also insisted Claire and she wear flip flops in the shower of the hotel, and Claire was kind enough to agree. Margaret wondered if Claire's germaphobia was nature or nurture? When they got into the hotel room, the first thing to go was the comforter. Even in a five-star hotel, Margaret was suspicious of whether they were really cleaning that thing between each guest. One could never know. Into the top of the closet it went. Followed by a good hand-scrubbing.

She was a bit neurotic about her health. She made many frantic phone calls to her dad, a paediatrician, when medical questions arose. Once, she had horrifyingly stepped into a deep puddle full of *who knows what*. Claire insisted it was just rain water, but Margaret could not be reassured. She had called her dad and although it was humiliating to relay the message that her underwear had gotten soaked when the puddle had splashed her, she couldn't enjoy the day without his reassurance. He laughed and told her not to worry — they would know in a couple weeks if she'd picked up anything — which was not reassuring in the least. She knew her mom and dad would have a good laugh, but when Margaret became afraid she was not rational. At the time of the puddle incident, she was still a bit uneasy about the man who'd been in the seat in front of her on the plane. He had turned his head to sneeze and had sneezed Cheetos all over Margaret's tray table. She had turned in horror to Claire, who took pity on her mother, scrubbing every surface with the sanitizing wipes she carried in every bag thanks to her mom. Margaret was, undoubtedly, a mess to travel with. She was actually just a mess overall.

Even back then, before going back to school, she loved hearing the French people speak. She loved saying *bonjour* when she entered a shop. She learned in her extensive research that it is considered very rude not to say hello when entering a store in France. This supposedly originated because stores used to be part of people's homes.

Margaret loved the way every French word looked and sounded. She smiled seeing *Patisserie* above the bakeries and *Boulangeri*e above the bread shops. Her vocabulary may have included twenty words, but she found herself craving more. She begged Claire to stop at every real estate listing posted in the city windows, looking at the prices and photos of the apartments, make-believing they were in the market. Which *quartier* would they live in? They would discuss the pros and cons of each one. The 8th and the 18th were out. Only for the extremely wealthy. That left eighteen others. The 20th was still a bit rough. Seventeen to go. They finally decided the left bank was for them. The Latin Quarter or Saint Germaine. Affordable as long as you could be content in five hundred square feet on the fifth floor with no elevator. It sounded perfectly perfect to them. Both knew that this was an unrealistic dream. They had lives back in America, with responsibilities and friends and family. The list went on and on as to why one couldn't always have what one wanted.

Now, as she embarked on her new path as a French student, she had a serious problem. So much time had passed since her last flight and the infamous on board panic attack, which had come to be known in her family as, "the incident." The fear of flying tended to grow when too long went between trips. Typically, the family took at least one vacation a year. They were one of *those* families where the divorced parents travelled together. Not ideal, but again, FOMO at work. There was also a series of years where Margaret had to travel for work; sometimes California, sometimes Chicago or Seattle.

But in the last few years Margaret's work kept her in the office and the kids were busy with their own lives. Margaret knew herself; the more time that passed, the more her fears grew. This was as true with dentist appointments as it was with giving presentations at work, and of course, with flying. She tried to convince herself that Greenwich was so well situated that she could go plenty of places by train. New York City was just a hop, skip and a jump away, as was Boston. She could easily visit Claire at NYU and Joseph in D.C.

without ever getting on a stupid plane. The mountains and the ocean were right there. She really did live in a wonderful place. Greenwich had been a perfect place to raise the kids. It was rather a small town, only about sixty thousand people, but it had all the great restaurants and shops due to all the tourists that flocked there during the summer. She and the kids spent their summers swimming. Right on the coastline, it boasted many beaches, but she loved Greenwich Point Park best, because not only did it have long stretches of sandy beaches, but there were miles of walking trails and a striking view of the New York City skyline.

Margaret had been adamant about the kids learning to sail. Her dad had been in the Coast Guard and they had lived in New London, Connecticut for years. He had taught her to love sailing — even though much of the sailing had been yelling at her to pull in this sail, no not that one. Now hurry or they were going to capsize! Tie this knot, no, not *that* knot — and she had passed that love on to her kids. As memories have a habit of becoming, these were now endearing stories she cherished. The kids were much better sailors than her because she had enrolled them in sailing school every summer. Plus, she was smart enough not to teach them herself and thus not to have to be the one to yell out commands. Most importantly, they had the fearlessness of youth. Margaret did not like to capsize, while the kids thought it was the greatest thing ever. Every time she went sailing with them, they capsized on purpose just to watch her come sputtering up, spitting sea water. They told her it was good practice, but could not say it with a straight face.

So, with all these amazing things at her back porch, she could easily justify to herself that she didn't really need to fly. She'd travelled enough, why leave? Deep down though, it bothered her that this fear controlled her.

She had been afraid of flying for years now (how anyone was not afraid to fly confounded her), but it had turned into a full-fledged phobia over the last two years. Suddenly, it seemed that stories of planes falling from the skies, often mysteriously and horrifically, were flooding the news. According to her therapist, these stories didn't actually flood the news, rather they flooded her mind.

"Margaret, I know these stories are upsetting," Dr Montgomery had assured her, "but they only make the headlines because they are extraordinarily rare. If crashes happened all the time, they wouldn't be all over the news."

"So you admit that plane crashes are all over the news?"

Dr Montgomery called this deflecting. Margaret called it being right.

Though she had, in fact, made quite a bit of overall progress in therapy, her fear of flying did not budge, and after the incident she had no plans of leaving the ground any time soon. Now, shame flooded her body when she thought about the fact that, disastrous flight to Maine aside, she hadn't left a fifty-mile radius in over three years. She pictured herself growing old in her little house, leaving less and less often as her fears got the best of her.

Needless to say, when she fed Dr Montgomery the "I quit my job to study French so that I can travel!" line, 'he simply lifted her eyebrows at Margaret as if to say, "you're not fooling me, kid'.

"Okay, I know what you're thinking," Margaret blurted out. Dr Montgomery could always get Margaret to talk without saying a word.

"I want to know what you're thinking," the doctor responded.

"Okay. I'm thinking that you're thinking that I'm either having a mid-life crisis or I'm totally full of shit about this whole thing."

"So which one is it?" Dr Montgomery replied calmly.

"Well, I am mid-life and I do love a good crisis!"

No reaction from the doctor. The woman should seriously consider taking up poker. She sat patiently while Margaret looked around the room to avoid eye contact. It had been fairly easy to open up about David, their divorce, her many anxieties, but for some reason this subject felt exceptionally personal.

"Dr Montgomery," she started when she could no longer bear the silence, "there is most definitely a possibility I will at some point have a mid-life crisis.

But that's not what this is. I have dreamed of studying French since I was a young girl, and at this point in my life the only thing I have to lose, is my pride, and I've certainly lost it plenty of times before."

After that, the honesty just poured out of her.

Chapter 5

Margaret found herself explaining to Dr Montgomery how she had desperately wanted to study French literature in college, and how her parents had told her that if they were going to pay for their daughter to get an education, she was going to get herself a useful degree. Her mother had teared up when she told her how lucky she was to have the opportunity, as a woman, to study things like medicine and law. So that's what she did. At enrolment, she wrote 'Political Science' under 'Major' and never turned back.

But with age, her parents had softened. Late one evening the previous year, long after her father had dozed off, she and her mother were up having tea in the kitchen. She loved visiting her parents. There was such a comfort in being under the same roof as the people who loved and protected you as a child.

"I hope I didn't make a mistake, pushing you to study law," her mother said suddenly.

Margaret gazed at her mother, still beautiful at seventy. She had perfectly creamy skin, light blonde hair that had never greyed, and hazel eyes that she and Margaret shared. In her teenage years when Margaret was often self-conscious, she would catch herself being envious of her looks. Margaret had thick, auburn hair that people complimented all the time, but in her younger years she had wished it could be blonde and perfectly smooth like her mom's.

Her mother had the gift of listening intently to whatever someone was saying. Margaret did not have this gift. She was always thinking of what to say next, while she should have been listening to the person talking and enjoying the moment. They were wired differently, that was her excuse. But in reality, Margaret felt that her mom was just better with people and might actually be a better overall person.

She was so thankful for moments when Claire and Joseph reminded her of her parents. Her mom was sociable and her favourite thing in the world was a party. Her dad was easy-going and just happy to be along for the ride. Every five or so years for her 'special' birthdays, the whole family would try to talk her mom into a trip, but she always requested a party. Margaret would never want a party for her birthday. She hated being the centre of attention. She always requested a small family dinner somewhere special. She often wondered how she could be so different from her mom and yet so alike.

The kids were a combination. Joseph was definitely more of an introvert like her, yet he was comfortable talking to people. He had a quiet confidence about him that Margaret admired. Claire was somewhere in-between. Unfortunately for her, she inherited

Margaret's clumsy and nervous nature, but she was also blessed with a quick wit and could make anyone laugh. She loved being with people, yet, like Margaret, she needed alone time to recharge.

Margaret returned her focus to her mother who was patiently awaiting a reply.

"Oh, Mom, I know you and Dad just wanted what was best for me," Margaret replied sympathetically. She really did know that, despite wishing they had supported her in her dreams. Still, at forty-five, Margaret could not imagine a life without her mother and panicked whenever the thought of losing her arose. It would give her a stomach ache when she let the thought grow and simmer. She was continually begging God for more time with her parents.

"It's just that you work so hard, and you do an incredible job, but well, I'm your mother and I know when you're experiencing genuine joy and when it's forced."

Margaret could hear that her mother was getting choked up, so she reached out and tenderly patted her hand.

"The kids are away at college now," her mother continued. "This is a new chapter in your life and I'd hate to see you spend any more time succeeding but not really enjoying it." Her mother dabbed her eyes and sighed. "Anyway," she said, clearing her throat, "getting older is strange. I've realized that most of what I thought was important when I was younger is really quite frivolous, and most of what I thought was frivolous is actually deeply important."

Margaret looked at her in wonder. Before she could utter a word, her mother kissed her on the head and said, "Off to bed, sweet girl," something only a mom would say to a forty-five-year-old divorcée with two grown children.

That night, unable to sleep, Margaret puttered around her childhood room. Her parents had spruced it up to use it as a guest room years ago, but they had kept her collection of globes displayed proudly on a pretty Lucite bookshelf that the interior designer told them would look chic in the bedroom, though she suggested keeping the globes elsewhere. They were kind of goofy, all different shapes and materials, but it brought Margaret comfort that her parents held on to them. Her mother also kept several nightgowns ironed and hanging up in the closet. It was old fashioned, yet such a sweet gesture that it almost made Margaret weep.

As an adolescent Margaret was fascinated with maps and globes. Along with her impressive globe collection, she had a big framed poster of the United States (which the designer discreetly moved from the bedroom wall to the walk-in closet). She had drawn a neat little star on each state that she visited, eighteen in total when she graduated high school and left home.

She smiled when she saw the one extra-large star stuck on the state of Georgia. She had begged her parents to go to any of the thirty-three states she hadn't yet visited the summer before college, in hopes of accomplishing her '18 by 18' goal that she had set as a hopeful twelve-year-old. She had written it neatly in her notebook, ages before the days of taking notes on your smartphone. They had already visited Hilton Head twice, but they were headed there again three weeks before her eighteenth birthday. She moped the whole way there, dramatically lamenting that '17 by 18' just didn't have the same ring to it.

On their last day of the trip, her father told the family he had 'wild hair' and was going to drive to Savannah for a day trip — and did anyone want to come along? Her mother, knowing full well what her father was doing, stayed behind with her older brother. Just Margaret and her dad took the hour-long drive. When they crossed the border into Georgia, he honked the horn and they both cheered. She remembered so clearly getting back home and drawing that big star right in the centre of the state, so proud of accomplishing her little goal. So grateful for her father's kindness.

Suddenly, her heart began to ache, as it often did when she felt nostalgic. The memory was so sweet, but also such a long time ago. She wondered if that spirited young girl was still inside of her somewhere.

Growing up, her parents had been great about taking her on vacations. They were both very much into education, so a trip to Florida, for example, had to include a stop somewhere in the south to view a particularly important Civil War site. Or a trip somewhere drivable just outside Connecticut might include a stop at one of those places that re-enacted the first settlers. Margaret rolled her eyes when talking about these excursions with her friends, but she secretly loved them. She and her parents were all three voracious readers, and the first thing they would look for any time they went somewhere new was a bookstore. They were all happy for a good hour or two picking out the perfect book for the trip. Her parents let her have pretty much all the books she wanted. Hence, her immense collection.

Each book brought back memories. She could tell you where she was when she first read *Anne of Green Gables,* and the summer she spent on the back porch reading *Gone with the Wind*. Her mom had put a few of Margaret's old favourites on her night table. *Winnie the Pooh*, because her grandmother had called her 'Pooh', when she was a little girl. *The Giving Tree* was there, which made her cry every time she read it, as well as *The Secret Garden*. There were no adult novels anywhere in sight, but luckily, she always had a book with her. She couldn't read scary books at night. She wouldn't sleep a wink; those were reserved for the daytime. But she had been wanting to read *Bel Canto* for ages and couldn't wait to begin. She cracked it open, hoping her mom had not already read it, because part of the fun of finding a great new book was sharing it with her.

She resolved to buy a new map and hang it on her study wall as inspiration. A map of the world this time. She would mark the places she had already been, when she was a child, and perhaps the courage to face down her fear of flying would begin to emerge. Margaret had to remind herself that her courage was still there somewhere, buried deep down inside of her.

Chapter 6

Two weeks later, Margaret was out feeding the stray cats behind the gas station, a nightly routine which she had only missed twice in the last year, once, when she had the stomach flu and then the other when she was in New London staying with her parents. She was so caught up in her childhood memories that she had completely forgotten to text Sara, her house sitter, who was the only other animal-lover sweet enough to agree to feed the strays in Margaret's absence. She didn't dream of telling her family about this tradition, who would either ridicule her, like David or Claire might, or berate her for going to a shady alley alone at night, which Joseph most definitely would do. He often worried about his mother's decision-making skills, and rightfully so.

She knew it was ridiculous to buy cat food every week for these strange cats, but she couldn't stop now. They counted on her. So she would open the bag of cat food and spread a long line down the alley. Cats would come from everywhere. They were no longer afraid of her and they now devoured the food without even looking up. A few had gotten brave and come close enough for her to pet them. She wanted to take them all home, but also did not want to become a cat lady. So this seemed to work for her, although she struggled worrying about them some days. Especially hot days. And more than a handful of her lunch hours had been spent lugging bags of ice to the water bowls she left out to make sure the water was cool enough. But sitting here for twenty or thirty minutes in the early evening brought her a strange sense of peace and a feeling that although she could not do much in the world, she could at least do this. She thought of a quote by Gandhi, "Whatever you do will be insignificant, but it is very important that you do it." This small act mattered to these cats.

Margaret was watching Raoul, a scrawny orange Tabby who she was particularly fond of, enjoy his dinner when she felt her phone buzz in her pocket. Her breath caught in her chest when she saw *Hartford Women's Health* on the screen.

"Ms James?"

"Yes?" Her voice cracked and she cleared her throat. "This is she."

"This is Sheila at Doctor Bronson's office. I'm calling about your mammogram results."

Oh god. What is it her doctor always told her? No news is good news?

"Doctor Bronson recognized some irregularities and she would like you to come in for a biopsy. She can squeeze you in tomorrow morning if you're available."

Results. Irregularities. Biopsy. Margaret heard the words but couldn't process them.

"Ma'am?"

"Yes, sorry. Tomorrow? Um, okay."

"The doctor can see you when our office opens at eight. Thank you, have a nice night." The phone line clicked and Margaret was left holding her phone in one hand and a bag of cat food in the other. Not knowing what else to do, she continued feeding the hungry cats as she tried to steady her breath.

When she got home, Margaret set her purse on the counter and bent down to scratch George on the head as he rubbed his body against her leg and purred. She opened a bottle of wine and took a slow sip, trying to gather her thoughts.

Suddenly, her cosy little cottage felt incredibly big and empty. She could call David, but that would only worry him, which wasn't fair. This kind of thing was not his problem any more. She thought about texting Beth, but knew she'd immediately start a separate group text, rallying all of her girlfriends together for support. Margaret didn't think she could handle all of that attention.

She looked at George who was weaving in and out of her legs, still purring.

Who will take George if I die? she wondered. She took another sip of her wine and then let out a laugh. *The only thing I'm worried about is who will take my cat if I die. I have reached peak pathetic-ness.* She downed her glass of wine and crawled into bed, carefully going over several worst-case scenarios in her head as George slept soundly beside her.

Exhausted the next morning, she found herself sitting on the crunchy paper of the examination table at Dr Bronson's office.

What an idiot she had been, certain she'd be taken down by a fiery plane crash or natural disaster, ignoring the much more likely possibility that she would get sick and die a lonely spinster.

"So," Dr Bronson said, interrupting her train of thought. "The results of the biopsy should take about three to five days. I'll call you as soon as I know anything."

Margaret was nodding, trying to look calm.

"And Margaret?"

"Yes?"

"Try not to worry. There's no reason to think about the worst-case scenario here, okay?"

Way ahead of you, Doc.

"Absolutely. Good thoughts only!" Margaret chirped. As soon as Dr Bronson was out of sight she typed 'FINALIZE WILL' at the top of her to-do list on her phone.

Despite it being an especially busy work week, time dragged out as Margaret awaited the dreaded call from the doctor. Every time her phone buzzed, she jolted, only to see that it was her mom or a telemarketer calling. She didn't dare tell her family yet; they'd have enough to worry about once she got the official word that she was, in fact, dying.

Finally, on Friday morning as she was sitting in her firm's weekly meeting, Margaret got the call she had been dreading all week. She quietly excused herself and answered the call.

"Margaret?"

"Yes?"

"This is Doctor Bronson. I have good news for you. Your biopsy came back negative."

"I'm sorry, what?" Margaret was baffled.

"The results were negative. Everything looked just fine."

"I'm okay?"

"You are. So we will plan to see you next year for your annual mammogram. Okay?"

"Next year. Sure. Thank you, Doctor Bronson." She hung up the phone and stood silent for a moment.

Instead of re-entering the meeting, Margaret walked to her office and shut the door. She sat in the middle of the floor and tried to process this news — this *good* news. She did not have to tell her family she was dying. She did not have to beg Sarah the house sitter to become legal guardian of George. She did not have to find someone to feed the strays behind the gas station in her absence.

She looked around her office, as if it was the first time she'd seen it.

"What the fuck am I doing here?" she said out loud to no one.

Before she could stop herself, Margaret grabbed the few puny personal items she had scattered around her office in the last twenty years, a framed photo of her children and another one of George; a little potted succulent; and the novel she was currently reading, which she typically read at her desk during lunch when she wasn't feeding the cats.

She held tightly to these items in her arms as she left her office, went down the elevator and walked out of her building once and for all.

She did go back later that afternoon to tell her director that she would be leaving. He was a nice guy and she wasn't a total asshole. But the feeling of walking out of that door and finally giving herself permission to do what felt right left her on a high for weeks. And the feeling of genuine relief made her confident that she was making the right decision.

The next morning, Margaret stayed in bed until nine a.m. snuggling with George. She sometimes thought of George as her best friend. He followed her everywhere and loved nothing more than riding around the house wrapped around her neck. If she had a nervous meltdown or was crying, George was distraught. He would lick her face and nuzzle her until she stopped feeling sorry for herself. He always made her feel better.

Margaret would be meeting later that day with Jessica, an ambitious young attorney at her firm who would be taking over her position. Jessica seemed genuinely passionate about her job and she would be a better fit than Margaret ever was. With George asleep on her feet, she got out her laptop and clicked 'apply online' on her local university's website. It didn't take long to complete. She had bookmarked the page and pre-filled out the application two years ago and named it 'someday'.

'Go back to school' had been on her list for years. Finally, between her conversation with her mother and her recent health scare, she knew that neatly storing things away for her future would get her nowhere. It was time to take action, even if it felt risky. "What do I want most in life?" she asked herself. The answer came quickly. She wanted to learn French and she wanted to go back to France.

And so, she found herself as a single, unemployed, middle-aged college student. On paper, it sounded cliché. Quitting her job to pursue her passion. It was not something she could logically explain. But she felt deep in her bones she had made the right decision. She could have easily plodded along at her job for twenty or thirty more years. And it wouldn't have been bad, but she would have had regrets. And regrets were what she was trying to avoid. 'What do I want most in life?' This question kept presenting itself to Margaret, over and over. Of course she wanted to be a good mother, and friend. A good daughter and a decent person. She did want those things. But how did she want to spend this precious second half of her life? After years of mothering and working and doing everything she was supposed to do. It was her life after all. Only she could decide.

When she finished recounting these memories to Dr Montgomery, she closed her eyes and let out a sigh of relief. When she opened her eyes again, they were filled with tears. As Dr Montgomery pushed the tissue box towards her, Margaret realized that this was the first time she had ever cried in therapy. She needed George. She was bringing him to therapy next time.

"Sorry, this is very unlike me," Margaret sniffled. She despised crying in front of other people. Don't cry in public was always on her list.

"There's no need to apologize. Expressing your true emotions is healthy," Dr Montgomery replied with a smile. She seemed genuinely pleased. "I don't know what this new life change is all about, but you're definitely doing something right."

She was. She knew she was. But it was still scary.

Chapter 7

To her surprise and delight, it wasn't just her passion for French that made Margaret's time in school enjoyable. As it turned out, her classmates were incredibly kind and welcoming. Nobody seemed to mind being her partner during group activities and no one seemed to mind sitting next to her. They asked her about her children, about what she was reading (her perpetual early-ness taught her to bring a book with her everywhere she went) and they were all intrigued about the story of quitting her job and becoming a student again in her forties. She guessed she was something of a novelty.

Three weeks into that first semester she even received an invitation from her classmate, Katie, to join her book club. Katie was the only other 'adult' in class, if being twenty-four really counted as being an adult. She had taken a particular interest in Margaret's book recommendations, but the invitation was still unexpectedly sweet.

"I can't believe these kids actually want to hang out with someone my age," Margaret said, laughing on the phone with Claire. She had her on speakerphone while she got ready for the club's first meeting of the season.

She usually avoided attending events with strangers like the plague, but there was no way she would pass up an opportunity to discuss books. She held the phone out so Claire could help her pick out what to wear.

"Mom, you are super cool!" Claire said enthusiastically. She was such a sweet girl. She never really went through the, *my parents are so embarrassing* phase. Suddenly Margaret missed her tremendously, but there was no need to say it. She'd certainly failed countless times as a mom, but her children never had to doubt how much she loved them. It had been apparent in every lunchbox note, every bedtime snuggle, and now every *I love you!* or *Good luck on your test!* text message. She swallowed the lump in her throat, said goodbye, and headed out the door, surprising herself yet again for choosing to spend an evening with complete strangers rather than nestled up at home with George.

Margaret felt a glimmer of excitement as she pulled up to the cosy French restaurant where she and Claire loved to grab breakfast. There was little she enjoyed more than reading and discussing books, and though she and her girlfriends technically had a monthly book club, it had become much more of a drink-wine-and-talk-about-everything-but-books club. Margaret skipped it half the time to stay home and read in bed.

She walked through the door holding her hardback copy of the book the group had chosen. It was a gripping psychological thriller, and Margaret had flown through it. Although she felt a little lame bringing the book with her, she decided she would rather be over-prepared than under. What if this was (fingers-crossed) one of those intellectual groups where people had dog-eared pages and underlined quotes? She wanted to be able to keep up.

Scanning the little bistro, Margaret thought about how this place was a great choice, a place she frequented herself. She loved the simple menu with perfectly curated wine pairings. She could tell quickly that Katie wasn't there yet. Margaret was, per usual, five minutes early, so it wasn't a surprise that her friend hadn't arrived. Seated at the restaurant were two older women at one table and a couple on a date at another. In the back, there was a group of five young people, chatting and ordering drinks. This was clearly her crew.

Margaret typically hated scenarios where she was required to converse with complete strangers, but her newfound confidence and excitement to discuss the book masked most of the awkwardness she felt. Katie had assured her that everyone was thrilled to add another member, especially one as well-read as her.

The group consisted of three young women, around Katie's age, and two men not much older. They were all laughing about something (Margaret hoped she hadn't missed much of the book discussion) so she politely sat down without interrupting.

As their laughter died down, Margaret started to feel a sense of unease. Why was no one addressing her?

Sure, these people are young, but they know how to introduce themselves, especially when they're expecting a new group member. Deciding it was up to her to make the first move, Margaret placed her book on the table and smiled hopefully at the five strange faces who seemed to be looking anywhere but at her. Beginning to panic, Margaret started sliding the book closer and closer to the centre of the table, giving everyone a chance to realize who she was.

One minute passed. Then two.

"Um, hello," one of the young men finally muttered.

"Hello there!" Margaret said, a little too enthusiastically.

Silence.

"I'm Margaret… Katie's, um, classmate?"

The group looked at one another nervously.

Margaret felt full-blown panic now, and in her usual fashion, she began speaking faster and faster.

"I'm sorry, did she not tell you I was joining your group? I, uh, I'm in her French class and she invited me to join your book club."

"Book club?"

Oh no.

"Are you all friends of Katie Jansen?"

The group once again exchanged glances and everyone began to shake their heads apologetically.

"Oh goodness," Margaret said, feeling her cheeks flush as she snatched her book off the table. Her chair wobbled behind her as she abruptly stood to leave.

"I... I could have sworn you were my group. I'm so sorry — carry on!"

She tried to act nonchalant as she smiled and waved goodbye. Margaret jumped in her car and fumbled through her purse for her phone. 7:07 p.m. Surely at least one group member would have been there by now. Had she made the whole thing up? Was she losing her mind? Maybe she had a brain tumour or dementia.

She searched frantically through her texts for Katie's name, scrolling to their conversation about the book club. There it was.

Okay, so we'll see you Wednesday night @ 7!

She double checked the date on her phone.

Tuesday.

Margaret started the car and drove home trying to decide if she should tell Katie's book club this horrifying story tomorrow night as a kind of ice breaker. Maybe they'd find her endearing and relatable, although she'd probably omit the brain tumour bit.

Of course, they might also find her forgetful and kind of sad; single, middle-aged woman gets invited to youthful book club and shows up on the wrong date, only to come crawling back the next night. Should she just call it a wash, and skip the book club altogether? No, she couldn't do that. Katie had been so kind to include her, and Margaret hadn't been able to hide her excitement. It would be impossible to cancel now.

It only took her the four-minute drive home to decide that, yes, she would drag herself back to the scene of the crime tomorrow. But she was definitely going to keep this blunder to herself. Even Claire would find it too cringeworthy.

The next evening, Margaret found herself at the same place, same time, ready for yet another potential humiliation. However, to her surprise, this time she walked into the restaurant with ease. Margaret spent most of her life worried about embarrassing herself. But despite her best efforts, she embarrassed herself all the time, so what was the use of all that worrying? The worst possible scenario had already occurred last night, and she survived.

In a stroke of luck, Katie was already seated with another girl when she walked in, and upon seeing Margaret she waved enthusiastically. The rest of the group arrived promptly, and to her delight, Margaret discovered that Katie had been telling her the truth about their excitement to have a new member, particularly one who actually read the book and was eager to discuss.

The five of them snacked on a charcuterie board and sipped French wine, first delving into the book of the month and then moving on to other great books they had read that year, and those that they were hoping to read next. Margaret wrote down some that sounded interesting to her, and she was flabbergasted in the best way to see that others were doing the same.

Everyone in the club had an impressive reading list, but no one could hold a candle to Margaret. Fortunately, in this group of book-lovers, her laundry list of completed books was seen as impressive and interesting, not at all *cat-lady-ish*, something Claire regularly warned her she was in danger of becoming. She tried to down-play her impressive book collection, by saying that she was a lot older than the others, therefore she had had a lot more time to read all these books.

Had she found her people? She pondered the thought later that night as she curled up in bed with next month's book choice, which incidentally she already had in a pile of to-be-read books. She had a tradition of sending her mother every good book she read. Seven stars or above, she passed it on. So she and her mom had a kind of mini book club themselves. She would write a note inside the cover, telling her a bit about the book and why she thought she would enjoy it. Of course, her mom treasured these books and had them stacked together in a bookcase just for the books Margaret sent her. If she loaned one to a friend, she was ruthless about making sure it got back to her. The funny thing was, since Margaret gave away all her best books, her own bookshelves were filled with the books that were good, but not excellent. Every once in a while, she literally had to go re-buy her absolute favourites because she liked to have a few shelves of her all-time favourites in case she wanted to re-read them. Plus, just looking at them brought back good memories. Margaret loved arranging and rearranging the books on her shelves. She always took the paper covers off and mostly liked to arrange the books by colour. It was a really pretty way to decorate, she thought. Another hindrance in her dream of moving to Paris was what in the world would she do about all these books?

A problem not worth worrying about, she reminded herself. She wondered if George would like Paris. She was trying to teach him a few commands in French. Seeing as he didn't mind the commands she gave him in English, she started with some simple words. He was smart, but learning a second language was hard after all. She showed him some flashcards of things she thought he might enjoy.

"*Souris,*" she said in a teacher-sounding voice, pointing to a picture of a mouse. "*Oiseau* means bird, George," and, "Okay, this one's easy, George, it looks and sounds like English." She pointed to a photo of three little bugs. "*Les insectes,*" she said smiling. She didn't feel the need to translate. George got it. Every morning, she let George have fifteen to twenty minutes of freedom in the backyard. She left the back door open, just in case he got scared and wanted to come back in. He had a set routine. Every single solitary morning, he came back in with a bug. *Un 99nsect.* He would then take it to his torture chamber, the mud room, where he would bat it about. Margaret was usually quick to rescue the bug and put it back out, but sometimes the poor little victim, was missing an antennae or a leg. She knew this confused George. He was so proud of his bugs. And he thought Margaret would be too. He had no interest in eating them. He was a man of more refined taste. He just wanted to play with them and chase them. So, George loved the pictures of grasshoppers, *les sauterelles*, and flies, *les mouches*, and they practiced each morning while Margaret had her coffee and George enjoyed his saucer of milk.

A thought occurred to her as she patted the space beside her, inviting George to settle in for the night while she read. What if she hadn't gone to book club tonight? She'd never know it, but she would have been missing out on an incredibly fun, fulfilling experience. 'Try new things', already on her list, got a star beside it. She then quickly added 'and get outside my comfort zone more often', before opening her fresh new book.

She loved a well-written novel's ability to transport her to another place and time. This story was set in 1920s' Russia. *A Gentleman in Moscow.* She was totally enchanted by the second page. A wealthy man in Russia was held prisoner in a five-star hotel for his crime of being wealthy. She could not wait to share this one with her mom. This would soon be added to her top twenty favourite books, another list she kept on her phone. Some books got dropped off the list to make way for others. It was always a challenge to keep the list at twenty.

Before letting herself become completely entranced by this new book, she thought about how she would be able to discuss it with her new club. Now, not all of her imaginary travels would be solo. Perhaps it would be a nice change of pace to take the journey with friends.

Chapter 8

Margaret was relishing her new-found freedom. She finally had the gift of time, which was the kind of luxury that money could not buy. Little things like going grocery shopping were now enjoyable. Tasks like that used to be dreaded; she'd run through the aisles as fast as possible, grab some stuff that might come together as dinner, and rush home. Now, she leisurely strolled the aisles, no stress at all. Sure, anxiety was a pretty constant companion, but finally the burden of 'doing it all' had lifted. Plus, with the kids out of the house, she could eat cheese and chocolate for dinner without complaints or judgement.

As she passed by the cheese aisle one day, her eye caught the name *The Laughing Cow*. It pleased her to no end that her mind could now translate this into French. *La Vache Qui Rit*. It literally meant the cow who laughs. This was one of those moments where she let herself feel the pride at having learned something that was really hard. She wanted to turn to all of the other customers and tell them how to say each item in French, but didn't want to get kicked out of the grocery store for harassing customers. Her kids loved this cheese. She used to put it in their lunchboxes. She had planned on getting something slightly more sophisticated, but it was delicious and it reminded her of the kids' childhood. She put a box in the grocery cart. And then she added a second just for good measure. She picked up a baguette and bought a couple of squares of chocolate at the check-out lane and *voilà — le dîner.*

That evening, she got a call from Claire who was bursting with news to share. "Guess what?" she practically shouted.

Margaret's mind immediately spun the way it always did when she didn't know what was coming next. Did she elope with that kid she went on a couple dates with? Or did she drop out of school? No, she reminded herself, this was her daughter she was thinking about.

"Mom?" Claire interrupted her train of thought.

"Oh, sorry, sweetie, what was it?" Margaret held her breath.

"I signed up for French as a minor!" Even though Margaret couldn't see her she could tell she was smiling.

"What about your Spanish minor?" Margaret asked, despite her excitement.

"I thought it would be fun if we studied the same language," said Claire, and Margaret's heart melted as it always did when her children did something kind.

These kids, she thought. No one ever tells you that when your kids leave at eighteen parenting is not over. Not by a long shot. For better or worse, they are yours forever. Sometimes that was a pain in the ass, but the good far outweighed the bad, and today was one of the really good ones. She was so happy it made her giddy. "Oh Claire, I would just love that," she beamed. And she would.

Margaret breezed through Elementary French I and II and on to the intermediate level, but she was beginning to understand that it was going to take more than fifty minutes, four days a week, to truly master the language the way she dreamed of. Her grades were pristine, but her conversational skills were shaky at best. She'd been studying for two years, and it was time to dig deeper. She had begun to buy children's books in French, hoping to gain some new vocabulary. She loved the adorable *Le Petit Nicolas*, which was kind of like a French *Dennis the Menace*. And of course, there was *Babar*, the sweet elephant who went from living in the jungle to living with an old lady in Paris. She was also enchanted with an old fifties-era series called *Martine*, which she discovered by chance at an estate sale. There were probably fifty *Martine* books, and despite the fact that they were children's books, there was always new vocabulary in each one. Reading certainly helped her vocabulary increase. She was translating less and less and simply reading in French. It was thrilling.

She also started to listen to some French music, hoping to improve her accent. Joe Dassin's catchy *Les Champs-Elysées* would be stuck in her mind for a month. And she loved *Soul Man* by Ben l'Oncle Soul.

There were beautiful songs sung by Céline Dion and classics like Edith Piaf. But despite all of her efforts, progress was really slow.

"I'm thinking of getting a tutor," she announced to her professor one day after class. She had grown fond of Madame Hansen and genuinely appreciated her enthusiasm and encouragement. With that said, she was a full-time professor and mother who only had so much to offer a middle-aged student who still couldn't pronounce *heureux* (happy) to save her life. That damn word. She always had a question to ask her professor after class, but tried really hard to remember that, unlike Margaret, she had a very busy life.

"I think that would be a wonderful addition to your studies," Madame Hansen remarked. "It just so happens that I have a suggestion for you, a tutor, but I'll warn you that she's tough."

"Madame Hansen, I think tough is what I need at this point," Margaret replied.

Madame Hansen scribbled out an email address on a post-it note, and passed it to Margaret. "*Bon courage*," she said, patting Margaret on the back.

Margaret opened the door to Bistro V, a busy, bustling restaurant and bakery in the heart of the city. She loved this place, mostly because it was a French inspired restaurant serving croissants and éclairs, petit fours and quiche. And she loved the outdoor seating. She felt much more apprehensive to meet her tutor than she had been to meet her professor on the first day of class. Madame Hansen was warm and friendly and, frankly, Margaret was her star student. Margaret's over-achieving nature was a stark contrast to the average college student who rarely did their homework and scrolled through their phone under the desk throughout class.

Celeste was a different story. "She's very… *French*," Madame Hansen had told Margaret.

"Well French is good," Margaret replied warily.

"She is certainly an expert on the language, and students who stick it out with her improve drastically, but like I said, she's tough."

Madame Hansen's words rang through her mind as Margaret approached Celeste, who was reading a novel in French at one of the back tables. She was a beautiful woman, striking really. She was thin. *Aren't all French women?* And stylish. *Aren't all French women?* She had on Audrey Hepburn style cigarette pants, a white silk blouse, and black ballet flats. A thin gold chain with a small C hung delicately around her neck, and she had several gold bangles on her wrist. Simple pearl earrings completed the ensemble. Such an easy outfit to put together, but Margaret was pretty sure it would not look as great on her. Margaret vowed to at least make an effort to put on some jewellery the next time she went out. Her age was hard to tell (Margaret was terrible at this anyway), but she was probably what the French called '*une femme d'un certain âge*'. This usually meant a woman in her fifties. She had a beautiful tan complexion and black hair tied back in a loose ponytail. She had on very little makeup except for her red lipstick, which was incredibly striking on her but Margaret assumed she knew this. This was a woman men would still stare at and who would be beautiful her entire life. Lucky her. *Elle a de la chance.*

"Celeste? Bonjour, je m'app—" Margaret was immediately silenced when Celeste raised her slender index finger, never taking her eyes off of her book.

Margaret felt like a scolded child as she stood awkwardly waiting for Celeste to finish reading. When she finally lifted her eyes from her novel, it was to look Margaret up and down.

"May I help you?" Celeste asked in a thick French accent.

"Um, yes, I'm Margaret."

Celeste blinked.

"We spoke briefly via email," Margaret continued, feeling more and more judged by the second. "I'm a student of Madame Hansen's and she recommended I reach out to you for tutoring."

Nothing.

"I… I think you replied that I could meet you here on Tuesday at nine?" Margaret's statement came out more like a question as she glanced at her watch. 8:59 a.m.

"Ah yes," Celeste responded, sounding bored. "Well, I must tell you that I am really only taking serious students at this time."

"Right," Margaret said, beginning to feel annoyed. "Like I said in my email, I quit my job last year to become a full-time French student. My children are grown, I have no romantic life and most nights I am at home studying with my cat. I doubt you have any more serious clients than me."

Celeste's expression did not change, but she started moving her pile of books and miscellaneous papers from the chair across from her. Margaret sat down, feeling frumpy in what just this morning was an outfit that she had loved. She had carefully picked it out wanting to look casually professional. Of course she didn't have many clothes left to pick from, but she thought her cream coloured sweater, white jeans and brown suede ankle boots were somewhat chic. However, next to Celeste, she felt chunky and not at all *haute couture*.

"All right," Celeste said.

Margaret had either intrigued her or broken her down with all of her jabbering. She didn't really care which one it was.

"Have a seat. *Commençons*. Let's begin."

Chapter 9

Margaret loved working with Celeste. It was utterly exhausting, but so beneficial. Unlike Madame Hansen, who let it slide when the students slipped back into their native English, Celeste absolutely insisted that only French be spoken. Margaret felt like she had to use every ounce of her brain to get through their forty-five-minute lessons. When she left, she was drained and her mind was swirling with French. She often found herself translating her thoughts into French. She'd be driving to the store thinking, *I need bread — j'ai besoin de pain.*

Six months into her work with Celeste, Margaret hit another snag. She remained far and away the best student in her French program at the university, but her conversational skills were still lacking. She met Celeste every Tuesday morning, and while the lesson was always gruelling, Margaret loved every minute of it. She finally felt that she could understand Celeste's incredibly thick Parisian accent, but coming up with the right words to reply continued to be painful.

The good news was that Celeste began to warm to her. It had taken months. For the longest time, she seemed cold and just going through the motions with Margaret. But now, she was coming up with different ways to help Margaret. She would lay a French word on the table and have Margaret come up with a sentence using the word. But the sentence could not be simple; oh no, she insisted Margaret use different verb tenses and be ready to expand the sentence. "The French are rigorous," she would say. Margaret assumed this meant that Americans were not. But as time went on, Celeste softened, and even joked with her. They often shared a laugh, maybe at Margaret's expense, but still, were they possibly becoming friends? Margaret hoped so.

"Celeste, do you have any advice for how to boost my vocabulary?" Margaret was afraid she would offend her tutor by asking, but she was probably already offending her by learning so slowly. Margaret was fearful that Celeste would drop her as a student if she didn't continue to make progress.

"*En fait, oui,*" Celeste responded before generously switching into English, something she rarely did these days.

"There is a group of men who I used to tutor, back when I was taking on just anyone," she said, seemingly brushing them off with a wave of her hand. "They have been learning for years, but they are certainly not advanced. They do really enjoy the language though. I believe they have a conversation group that meets on Thursdays."

As Margaret considered this suggestion, Celeste continued. "You would be the best speaker, but perhaps the extra practice would be good, *non?*"

Margaret took a moment to bask in the light of this rare compliment from Celeste before realizing that she was being advised to join a group of men who managed to be, despite years of practice, worse than her. So much worse, in fact, that Celeste had fired them as clients.

"*Ecoutez*," Celeste said, seeming to read her mind, "no one sets out to learn something new and becomes an expert in a year, even two or three."

Margaret smiled gratefully.

"But Margaret," Celeste said, raising her eyebrows, "perfection, that is not the goal. Listen to my English accent. I have been here twenty years."

Margaret had never thought about Celeste's thick French accent as anything but beautiful.

"You will have an accent. You will forget words. This is certain. But why care? This is not failing. These men? They will not ever speak French beautifully. But they will speak it better than their friends who never bothered to learn. Someone wise once told me, five years will pass, whether you learn something new or not."

Margaret was taken aback by this sudden pep-talk from her hard-ass tutor. "Celeste, of course you're right, but I am the definition of a perfectionist."

"You must forget this. Read, speak, play music, immerse yourself in French, but *enjoy*." She exaggerated this last word. "This is the French way."

And that is how, two days later, at seven a.m. sharp, Margaret found herself walking into a cosy local diner in search of three geriatric Francophiles. They were hardly difficult to locate; three elderly men speaking French — attempting to speak, that is — entirely too loud.

One man was wearing hearing aids, and another had on orthopaedic sneakers. *Good lord*, Margaret thought, *Celeste either thinks I belong with this motley crew because my French is atrocious or I look a hell of a lot older than I really am.* Margaret couldn't decide which was more offensive.

"*Les... œufs... goutent... bien*," one of the men was saying, pointing to his eggs.

"*Plus... len-te-ment...* Bernard!"

"I can't speak any more *lentement*, Arnold. Keep up!" They all burst into laughter, and Margaret smiled in spite of herself.

"Bonjour, madame," one of the men said, addressing Margaret. He was wearing a sport coat with sneakers, but still appeared to be the most pulled together of the three. "Are you the young lady that is to be joining our French club?"

Her ears perked up at the sound of *young lady*, something she hadn't been called in fifteen years.

"Yes, hello, I'm Marg—" a wrinkled hand in her face stopped her in her tracks.

"En français, s'il vous plait," one of the men said, cutting her off mid-introduction.

She couldn't help but smile, despite the obvious rudeness of the gesture. She'd heard these men speaking

French moments ago, and the thought that they were insistent on a 'no-English' breakfast was humorous, yet endearing.

"*Pardon*," Margaret said, playing along. "*Je m'appelle* Margaret." She tried to speak slowly and clearly, giving each of the men a chance to reply.

"*Bonjour, madame, je m'appelle* Bernard." Bernard was clearly the ringleader of this strange little club, and he took it upon himself to introduce the others in broken French. Bernard, it turned out, had been a doctor and after he retired, had been teaching up until three years ago. He was handsome for an older man. He was well dressed also. Actually, she loved the outfit he had on. He was wearing a collared shirt under his navy V neck sweater with tailored tan pants and very cool dark blue leather tennis shoes. Tall and slim, he was confident and exuded intelligence. His eyes sparkled with spunk. He was probably close to eighty years old, but he definitely still had it all together.

"*Il s'appelle* Arnold," Bernard stated, pointing to the man with the hearing aids.

Arnold had a warm smile that made his eyes crinkle, and when he took Margaret's hand in both of his, he offered her an enthusiastic, "*Enchanté, madame.*" Margaret knew instantly that she liked him. Arnold was the man you would want for your grandfather. He was slightly pudgy like a grandpa should be, but not overweight, just soft. He wore a nice cashmere cardigan, but Margaret noticed a little hole on one sleeve. Margaret wondered if he had perhaps lost the person who would have mended it, and the thought made her sad. She could adopt Arnold. She could feel his kindness and she wanted to get to know this man.

"*Et il s'appelle* Frank," Bernard gestured over his shoulder to the gentleman in the orthopaedic shoes. To Margaret's surprise, he seemed to bounce out of his seat to greet her.

"*Enchanté, ma cherie,*" he said, playfully kissing the top of Margaret's hand as if she were royalty.

"This one's a handful," Bernard laughed.

"*En français*, Bernard," Frank shot back, winking at Margaret.

She couldn't stop the thought that popped in her head. *This man looks exactly like a garden gnome.* It wasn't the kindest comparison, although gnomes were kind of cute. Frank was completely bald and probably more than a head shorter than her. He had glasses that made his eyes look really big and he had a scarf wrapped around his neck. She literally could plop him in her garden and he'd fit right in. All he needed was the cone hat. She mentally scolded herself for mocking him, even in her head. She was a firm believer that people should not be judged by their looks. At least that's what she told herself to feel better when she was having one of her bad hair days.

Frank looked up at her, and she felt like a giant. He was for sure going to be a handful just as Bernard had warned. She could feel him already flirting with her and even though he was her father's age and she should be able to laugh it off, it did make her slightly uncomfortable. She'd never really been comfortable receiving male attention, which definitely made dating a challenge.

"*Bonjour, mes nouveaux amis,*" Margaret replied warmly. *Hello, my new friends.*

Were these really her new friends? Frank immediately broke rank and started rattling in English about his workout routine. That's why he was so agile, he explained. And perhaps she may have noticed. (She had not.) And would she care to look at his abs? (She would not.) Not registering the disinterest on her face, he lifted up his shirt right there in the middle of the restaurant. Margaret couldn't look away. Honestly, it wasn't bad for a man of his age, and she made the mistake of complimenting him. Without taking a breath, he launched into a description of his home gym and how it was important to lift heavier weights with less repetitions. He also shared that he had recently taken up Pilates, which was really keeping him limber. Margaret didn't speak a word. She was still trying to process the fact that she was flashed by a senior citizen and her reaction was to compliment him.

Before Frank could go into detail about his newfound flexibility, Arnold swooped in and saved her. He told Frank, kindly, that their new friend was there to practice French and perhaps they should get to it.

When the waitress came to take their order, Margaret winced as they each took their turn speaking in slow, broken French. Then one of the others would interrupt and try to help them or criticize their accent or their order. "The cinnamon rolls aren't any good here, Bernard, remember?" Frank practically shouted.

The waitress was used to this ragged group. She didn't even speak French, for crying out loud, but she had a bemused smile on her face and Margaret appreciated her patience. And, to be fair, when it came time for her to order, Margaret struggled herself. She didn't know the words for eggs Benedict. Her new friends jumped right in to help her and soon they were eating and swapping stories and she had tears rolling down her cheeks, she was laughing so hard. They pelted her with questions. They all had mastered asking questions in French, so she did most of the speaking, trying to answer as fast as they asked. They were so interested in her. It really was sweet. She couldn't wait to tell her mom about her new crew. They were strange and slightly inappropriate and yet darling. She was pleased to have joined their group.

What a funny thought. If Margaret was being honest with herself, she would admit that she wasn't always open to the idea of new friends. Her two closest friends had been in her life since college, and between them, her kids, her parents and colleagues, she always felt like she didn't have room for anyone else. But, in reality this was an excuse. She didn't want to put the effort into making new friends. And she craved her time alone. It made her feel guilty (her most common emotion) since she knew there was nothing more important than people. But still, having too much time with others depleted her. She had to recharge with time by herself.

Now, since completely overhauling her life in the last two years, Margaret had made friends twenty years her junior, and here she was befriending strangers almost thirty years her senior. She found that these new relationships didn't actually take anything away from her. They added layers of whimsy and interest to her life, like the flaky layers of the perfect *mille-feuille*.

Thinking of *mille-feuilles*, Margaret decided she should most definitely stop by the bakery on her way home and treat herself to one. In fact, she would get a box for her new French group; her *nouveaux amis*. For the first time since she was in her twenties, Margaret actually considered whether buying expensive pastries was within her budget. She decided that this was a special occasion, so they most definitely were justified.

Since quitting her job, Margaret spent every morning the same way. She woke early — she'd always been an early riser — and instead of scrambling to get herself and the kids ready like she had for years, now she slid on her sneakers and headed out the door towards the greenbelt that spanned her neighbourhood. She used to run when she was in her twenties, but she never really enjoyed it, it was just a quick way to get some exercise.

Well, now she could walk. She could walk for an hour if she felt like it. She wished George were here to see all this beauty. He would appreciate it, but he might get lost. She had wanted to get him one of those cat leashes and take him for walks, but her family had the nerve to forbid her from ever becoming a woman who takes their cat for a walk. Margaret was still considering defying their orders.

Margaret adored where she lived. She had bought a small but comfortable cottage style home after her divorce that was just half a mile from the large house in which she and David had raised the kids. David had offered to let her stay in the family home, but she couldn't bear to take one more thing away from him. And secretly, she hated the thought of being in that big house alone while the kids were with their dad. So she purchased a three bedroom, two bathroom house on a block with huge oak trees that grew so tall, they almost formed a canopy over the street.

Before the kids left for college, she was thankful for the proximity to David's house. It was both convenient and comforting being nearby on the evenings they spent with their dad. At the time, she was really too busy to even appreciate the beauty of her surroundings.

But now, what she appreciated about her quaint neighbourhood was its lush green trees and sprawling parks that led to a small plaza that just so happened to house her favourite coffee shop. It was a mile away, which was the perfect distance, particularly since she had nowhere else to be. Margaret strolled leisurely past the large grassy area where young children kicked soccer balls, to the tree-covered benches where an elderly couple often sat in peaceful contemplation, until she reached the coffee shop, where she would order a hot coffee with steamed milk. Sometimes she sat on the patio and sipped her drink, and other times she took it in her travel mug back towards the park. The whole experience took her about an hour, an amount of time she couldn't fathom sparing just a couple years ago.

Being unemployed no doubt had its advantages, but Margaret was keenly aware that she was going to have to work again at some point. She'd been frugal her whole life. Aside from her love of coffee, books and good wine, she rarely spent money on herself. Her house was fully paid for and so was her car. Aside from splitting the kids' tuition with David, which she insisted on doing, her expenses were low. Sure, she owned some nice clothing, but she was hardly a 'shopper'. She'd saved religiously and was financially very stable, having more than enough in savings to last her for years. But the thought of dwindling down her life savings without a plan made her stomach flip. What if she lived to be a hundred or suddenly needed lifesaving surgery?

She was sitting outside of the coffee shop while she mulled over her plan of action. She knew she could fall back on her law degree — she could get a part-time job or do some freelance work — but she dreaded the thought of going back to that life. She wanted to find something she actually loved, the way she loved being a French student.

I could be a barista, she thought as she blew on her hot coffee. But Margaret immediately knew she would be a terrible barista; way too frazzled and clumsy.

Plus, would she actually have to clean the bathrooms? That would rule that profession out.

Margaret thought about her other interests. Maybe she could work at the wine and cheese shop she often frequented — they could barricade her behind the checkout counter so she wouldn't break anything. Or what about the bookshop? That might just be her dream job. Or the animal shelter? *Do they pay? Would it be really smelly?* Margaret's thoughts were swirling.

She took a deep breath and tried to slow her thinking. She decided not to rush in to anything, she would finish this semester, which would put her exactly halfway through her studies, and then pursue a part-time job somewhere. And yes, she reminded herself, at this point she could still afford the pastries for her classmates. And the Friskies cat food for her beloved gas station cats.

She couldn't help but fantasize about all of her dream careers on her walk home. Welder — this being spurred on by her obsession with *Flashdance*. It was probably not exactly an accurate portrayal of a welder. Bartender? Hm… any fear of becoming an alcoholic? Librarian? Once again, a love of books, but rather dreary and musty. Beekeeper? Yes, she loved bees and knew how important they are to our planet, but they did sting.

She stopped to set her coffee down so she could type 'Find dream job' on her list of goals.

Margaret was basking in her peace and quiet that evening when the doorbell rang. No one ever rang the doorbell, so she was frightened at first until she heard a familiar, "Hellooooo! Margaret? It's us!"

Oh shit.

It was her two crazy aunts. Her mother's sisters. She had always wondered how her mother could be so normal and her sisters so nuts. Margaret secretly knew that she herself could easily become these ladies one day. Her quirkiness could turn into craziness, so she attempted to keep her judgement at bay. She opened the door to two slightly overweight, grey-haired ladies, one with a purple streak in her long hair. They were practically bouncing on their toes with excitement at her surprise, and Margaret smiled despite herself. Margaret hated surprises, even from beloved relatives. Naturally, her first thought was, *How long will they stay*? They had surprised her before and stayed a weekend but they had also surprised her with a slightly traumatizing month-long visit. She was always anxious to lose her freedom even though she loved these crazy ladies most of the time.

The three sisters had always vowed to live together if ever their husbands died before them. Sadly, two of the three were now in that situation, but they seemed to have not missed a beat. She ushered them in, but they charged ahead, already knowing the way. Margaret snuck a glance at how big the suitcases were. It was hard to guess. Luckily each only had one, but they were on the large side. She would call her mom the first chance she got and beg for backup.

Meanwhile, she gave them big bear hugs and waited for them to get settled upstairs. Her mind raced. How would she study with them around? How would she find any peace? *Temporary*, she reminded herself. *It's only temporary.*

The aunts, Rosie and Bee, came bounding down the stairs. They were ageless. Bee rushed out to the garden without asking and sank down in a lounge chair shouting back, "Is it too early for wine?"

That was rhetorical, Margaret knew. She and Rosie went into the kitchen for some rosé. Aunt Rosie immediately jumped into how they could transform this kitchen. They could knock down that wall and make it more open. She had brought her tools.

Margaret gasped. She knew the open concept was what everyone wanted now, but she loved her little cosy rooms. She also knew Rosie was fully capable of knocking down a wall while she was gone, so she sternly told her, "No changes without my permission. I mean it, Aunt Rosie."

"Fine, fine" Rosie winked.

They carried the rosé out to the garden, where Bee was casually smoking a joint. "Aunt Bee!" Margaret shouted. "Not okay! Put that out! Right now!" She instinctively looked around to see if anyone was watching. What would her neighbours say if they smelled it?

Aunt Bee giggled, and for a moment looked much more like a teenager than a seventy-year-old. "Chill, Margaret, it's all the rage. Everyone smokes pot now."

"No, Aunt Bee, they do not. It is not 'all the rage'." Margaret had never smoked marijuana in her life. She was way too scared of getting in trouble or being out of control.

"Come on, Margaret, just once, for your Bee," her aunt begged. "Just one little bitty puff."

Oh, dear Lord, Margaret thought as she rolled her eyes.

"Aunt Bee, if I take one tiny puff, do you promise to throw all your weed out?"

"Sure, honey, I promise."

Bee had always been true to her word, and Margaret was pretty sure that if she didn't take action, Bee would be out in the garden smoking pot every day, and probably planting some too. She walked over to Bee and tentatively took the cigarette. She didn't even know what to call it. She took one inhale and coughed. "Just one more, Margaret," Rosie and Bee cheered, as if they were all college students daring each other. She took one more puff and then the next thing she remembered was laughing. They were all laughing uncontrollably about everything. Weren't the flowers funny? Wasn't her mother hilarious? Wasn't life just the best? Everything was comical. They danced and sang and told stories that normally would not have been funny, but they sure were tonight. The joint was passed and more wine was poured, and their stomachs ached from their fits of laughter.

Things did not feel at all comical the next morning. Margaret was horrified at herself. She had lost complete control of the aunts on night one. They had all fallen asleep on the lawn chairs, and the sprinklers had woken them up. That would have been humorous last night but this morning, all heads were hurting. They stumbled their way to their respective beds and slept till noon. Margaret missed class for the first time and she was fighting mad when the aunts finally came downstairs.

"There have to be rules, you guys," she said sternly. They were not exactly ashamed — they'd certainly done worse — but they were willing to admit they may have gone a wee bit too far. They reassured her that the weed had gone down the toilet, but if she wanted, they could get more. "No," she yelled. "This is a weed-free house. Is that understood?"

They nodded a bit sheepishly.

"Okay," Margaret said, softening a bit. "Thank you. I'm sorry I yelled. Now I'm going to go study. You two be good." She raised her eyebrows playfully at them. They encouraged her to go get her work done. They were perfectly content to have some coffee in the garden.

When she came back, hours later, they were planting peonies in her garden. It was a peace offering. Peonies had been her beloved grandfather's favourite flower and thus it was hers. She cried, for her aunts' kindness and for missing her grandad so much it hurt. They hugged and all was good in their world again. But it was even better when they left two days later.

Chapter 10

One morning, Margaret sat down with Celeste for their weekly meeting and was surprised when Celeste didn't jump right into her rigorous curriculum.

"Margaret," Celeste began, "I'm wondering if you would be interested in taking on some of my tutoring clients?"

Margaret was completely taken aback.

"*Moi?*"

"*Oui, bien sur.*" Celeste was always switching back into her native French, even outside of their lessons.

"I... I don't know. Do you really think I am qualified to tutor?"

Celeste took a deep breath. Margaret knew her lack of confidence annoyed Celeste to no end.

"Margaret, I am not recommending you for the Académie Française, I'm just seeing if you might be interested in working with some beginners." Celeste pulled off a chunk of her croissant and continued speaking before taking a bite. "People reach out to me all the time for tutoring. Plus, I'm overbooked as it is, you know, *je suis très occupée*," she said, popping the flaky pastry into her mouth. "Pas mal," she remarked with a little shrug.

Celeste was always comparing the food she ate to *la nourriture* in France. She seemed to be one of those mysterious French women who ate however she liked without gaining any weight.

Margaret mulled the tutoring offer over in her head while Celeste ate slowly, pausing now and then to have a sip of her coffee. Margaret certainly wouldn't call Celeste relaxed, but at the same time she never seemed to be in a hurry. She quietly allowed Margaret to think.

On the one hand, Margaret was not exactly a patient person. She worried she might get frustrated with one of her clients if they learned too slowly. But on the other hand, she loved French so much that it actually felt wrong not to share it.

She imagined teaching clients her favourite French poems and bringing them recipes for crepes that they could practice at home. It actually sounded magnificent.

"Okay," Margaret finally answered. "I'm in, under one condition."

"Oui, madame?"

"No way am I tutoring any kids."

Celeste gave a firm nod.

"And for the love of god, no single men."

"*Pas de problème*," Celeste said nonchalantly, "I'll email you the list of potential clients *tout de suite*."

Margaret smiled.

Celeste raised her coffee cup to toast Margaret, and they both said "*Tchin-tchin*," as they clinked glasses.

It wasn't until she left the café that it dawned on Margaret that she had just procured a paying job. Doing something she loved. She had been so focused on learning French that it hadn't occurred to her that she could actually teach it one day. She did a happy little jig as she strolled to her car, not caring that Celeste could see her out of the window.

As soon as Margaret got home, she began compiling resources to be used for tutoring. She'd accumulated quite a lot of books, of course, but also piles of short stories, activities and handouts. She figured that step one was to see what kind of students she was dealing with, so she opened up her email to find the list, as promised, from Celeste. Margaret found a list of five clients, each followed by brief descriptions.

Margaret noticed that there was one group of two. Next to their names Celeste had typed, *pushy older couple.* Margaret smiled. Celeste somehow simultaneously offended and charmed her. She pressed on to the next name, Patricia. Margaret's heart sank a bit upon reading her description — *smart but hopeless.* As a college student in her late forties, Margaret liked to believe, perhaps naively, that no one was hopeless. She decided that Celeste must have been particularly harsh with her critiques. It wasn't a far-fetched idea. A middle-aged, *hyperactive* man and a young, single woman who had recently reached out to Celeste for tutoring rounded out the list.

It sounded like a slightly pathetic bunch, and Margaret tried not to take personally the fact that Celeste seemed to always set her up with misfits. On second thought, though, Margaret actually didn't mind. She'd been a bit of a misfit her whole life and would much rather spend her time with flawed people than people who feigned perfection. No matter how terrible any of them were, Margaret vowed to appreciate this opportunity to teach. Plus, it was a paying job doing something that she actually enjoyed. She was eager to get started, so she began emailing the clients right away.

How would she word her emails?

Bonjour! I'm writing to let you know that you've been fired by your tutor, Celeste. I am a slightly-better-than-you client who will now become your instructor. A bientôt!
Margaret

Perhaps, here, brutal honesty was not the best policy. She began again.

Bonjour! My name is Margaret, and I am assisting Celeste with her tutoring business. I'm thrilled to begin working with you — please let me know when you would like to begin. A plus tard!
Margaret

She switched from her email to the essay she was currently writing, typing as she hummed along to Edith Piaf singing *La Vie en Rose* in the background. Margaret had researched the singer for one of her first assignments in her elementary level French class. She was, perhaps, France's most celebrated singer ever, but her story was absolutely heart-breaking. She was born in the 20th arrondissement, impoverished and basically abandoned by her parents. Her father once returned from a trip and found the child so malnourished that he took her to his mother, Edith's grandmother, who ran a brothel. That was the place where Edith grew up. She was given no attention, and at ten she considered herself completely on her own. She sang in cafés to earn enough money to survive. She was discovered and became wildly successful, but she was never truly happy. She had many marriages and did not enjoy the money she earned, giving it all away. France always called her 'their poor little sparrow'. Even though she never really felt it, she was deeply beloved, and forty thousand people showed up to mourn her at her funeral.

Margaret adored listening to her music while she studied, although the sadness and heartache were evident in her beautiful songs. Thinking about Edith's life reminded Margaret to count her blessings. She rolled her shoulders back and typed as the music played lightly in the background. To her surprise and delight, she received her first reply ten minutes later. It was from the couple:

Is tomorrow too soon? M & R

Margaret clapped her hands together in excitement. Tomorrow! They decided on eight a.m. at the coffee shop in her neighbourhood. Margaret tried to remember what she'd done with Celeste at their first meeting. Mostly she recalled being gently berated in French, but Celeste did have some great reading materials, and her French only policy was brutal but effective. Margaret decided she would take what she appreciated from Celeste's lessons and leave the rest. These clients were not majoring in French at a university, they just wanted to learn for pleasure. Margaret liked a plan, so she saved her essay and opened up a new document. She titled it *'Leçon* 1'.

Chapter 11

Margaret arrived twenty minutes early to set up for her first official clients. Yes, they were actually just Celeste's rejects, but she really couldn't care less about that fact. Celeste rejected almost everyone and she was just excited to be a real French tutor. She was, however, concerned about the 'pushy' note she had read about the couple. *Pushy how?* she thought. She tried to remind herself that she was the expert in this situation, no matter how bizarre that felt. Pushy or not, she was in the driver's seat.

Despite her mental pep talk, when Margaret introduced herself to the couple who arrived right on time and raring to go, she immediately felt as though she was being interviewed.

"Oh, hello dear," the woman said with a smile. "I hope you don't mind, but we brought our son along for the first lesson. His wife is French-Canadian and we thought he could help out if us old geezers need a little assistance," she said matter of factly.

Margaret inadvertently frowned. *Am I one of the old geezers or are you referring to yourself and your husband?* she wondered.

She tried to smile as she pulled out the lessons she had created, despite feeling a combination of panic and irritation. Was the son going to speak French better than she did? Why didn't *he* just tutor them if he was so good in French? However, it was quickly obvious that he was a reluctant participant in this strange scenario. The couple nudged him several times, prompting him to ask a question or two in French. Each time he gave Margaret an apologetic smile. She was terrified that at some point she would be found to be a fraud, but with great gratitude and thankfulness she was able to answer his questions. In fact, she answered them with ease. He excused himself halfway through the lesson, insisting his mom and dad would learn more without him distracting them. After that initial meeting, he never came again, and Margaret was eternally grateful.

She guessed she had passed their test, because the couple continued to show up eagerly for their lessons, week after week. Celeste had not been wrong about them being pushy, but Margaret still thought they were cute. Tutoring couples could be a bit tricky, because one was always going to be a bit better than the other. So, she tried to complement each one's strengths and make it fun for them. They may have been slightly bossy with her, but the way they encouraged one another made Margaret smile. They also had incentive to learn. Their son's children would be brought up speaking French and they did not want to be left out. When they showed up to their lesson one day a few months in, they were bursting to share with Margaret that their son's wife was expecting their first child. That next week, Margaret surprised them with a tiny onesie that read '*bébé*' and they beamed with pride and excitement.

Margaret's second client was named Patricia. Patricia was an incredibly smart physician who had quite possibly the worst French accent Margaret had ever heard. No amount of correcting would get her to pronounce *je* correctly, as in 'juh' and not as in 'jay'. Patricia's pronunciation wasn't her only hurdle, and it was difficult for Margaret to fathom how someone so intelligent could not comprehend the simple concept of conjugating a verb.

Nevertheless, Patricia was persistent, explaining to Margaret that she needed to be fluent in six months because she and her husband had an upcoming trip to France. Margaret wondered how she could explain to Patricia that even if she weren't the world's worst French student, no one could become fluent in six months. Margaret knew more than most that learning another language, especially as an adult, was a lifetime pursuit. Celeste had been wise to advise Margaret to let go the idea that having a perfect accent or remembering every word was absolutely necessary. She tried to lightly relay this same message to Patricia, while still remaining encouraging. Language came naturally to Margaret, as she imagined science did to Patricia. She tried to put herself in her student's shoes; picturing herself attempting to study biology or chemistry. She wouldn't become an expert in six months, or even in a year or two, but she could perhaps master some basics. This would be her approach with Patricia. Was Patricia going to be fluent when she went to France? No. But could she help her learn enough useful phrases and expressions to get by? Yes. *Well*, Margaret thought, *that's more of a solid maybe.* But she would give it her all.

They met twice weekly for six months, and when Patricia left for France, she could recite her hotel's address, ask directions and order at a restaurant in fairly comprehensible French. She even had a breakthrough and began pronouncing *je* correctly. Margaret saw this as a success, and felt a sense of pride when she received a smiling selfie from Patricia with a text that read, *Bonjour, mon amie*!

It did make her clients feel better when she said to them, "When you go into a hardware store, do you know the names of all the items, even in English?" Of course not. The same would always be true with French. Of course, people like Patricia felt like they were different, or smarter, and Margaret could tell that Patricia nodded her head in a way that meant, *we'll see.* After six months, Margaret had Patricia ready to go to France with some basic beginner's French, but luckily Patricia was ecstatic with her knowledge and had completely forgotten that she had thought that she would be speaking like a local at this time. Learning a second language was an incredibly humbling act.

When she got back from France, Patricia continued her lessons with Margaret. Margaret loved sharing her passion, but she also loved developing relationships with those she tutored. She felt a bit of pride that Patricia had first come to her to learn French solely for a trip, but had now come to love the language and wanted to keep her lessons up. Many of her clients were becoming good friends, and suddenly she was receiving postcards from their travels and getting invited to their birthday parties. This was not good for her new budget, but it was good for her soul.

Anna was the youngest of her clients. She was probably just a year or two older than Claire. Margaret was not quite sure if she was being paid to tutor Anna in French or to serve as an unqualified part-time therapist. Anna was almost thirty, but she had recently moved back in with her parents as she was in-between jobs. Margaret discovered quickly that she was always in-between jobs. This poor, young woman could not seem to get it together. Her parents had paid for her to get her master's in speech therapy, but after a year she realized she did not enjoy it. While that might be understandable, there had been three more failed careers after that. She had gone to hairdressing school, gotten her real estate license and was lately getting her yoga certification. Nothing was quite 'her'.

She came to her lessons every week, however, without fail. She always paid on time. And when she had to miss a lesson, she insisted on making it up that same week. She seemed so interested in learning French and she had been with Margaret every week now for over a year. They did spend sometimes half the lesson trying to get her life back on track, but Margaret would then gently guide her back to her French.

Recently, her parents had kicked her out, citing tough love, and Anna was on a friend's sofa. She had tears in her eyes the day she shared the news. It was, surprisingly, the first time Margaret had seen her truly upset. She really did want to get her life together. Without thinking it through, Margaret offered to let her live temporarily in one of her small guest bedrooms. Her kids were going to have a fit about this, but she couldn't take it back. Anna jumped up and hugged her and told her that she would be the easiest roommate ever. Roommate? Margaret was a bit old for a roommate. She was hoping this was more like, Anna would stay a week or maybe two while she figured things out. Anna lugged in three suitcases that very afternoon, along with a fish named Fred. *George will eat that thing within the week*, thought Margaret.

Surprising both of them, they were, in fact, good roommates. They were both considerate of one another and Margaret was gone all day anyway, studying or meeting with her French group, leaving Anna to do whatever it was that Anna did. Margaret sure hoped that she was looking for a job. She tried not to push her, but found herself suggesting jobs at the dinners they occasionally shared. Margaret could not help herself from occasionally offering to bring home dinner for both of them. She worried about Anna's health if she kept eating cheap food from McDonald's and Taco Bell. After a month of crashing, Anna had actually found a job in events at a museum. This was a good fit for Anna. She was great with people and didn't mind working odd hours. Margaret was so proud of her. She did hope, though, that Anna would start saving money for her own place. Margaret wanted her solitude back, but there was no way she could kick Anna out.

As predicted, Fred disappeared. Shockingly the fish bowl was still intact, not a drop of water spilled. But it was missing its resident. Margaret had warned Anna, but she still felt terrible. She was pretty sure Fred was already living on borrowed time, but he didn't deserve to be murdered. She tried to make up for it by bringing home Anna a hamster from the pet shop. It worked. Anna took to this hamster like it was her own little baby. She carried it around the house and showed Margaret all the things that Roger could do.

George looked on with great interest. Not too long after, Margaret found Roger in George's mouth. Margaret screamed and George dropped Roger, who thankfully was unhurt. George was quite adept at opening Roger's cage, it turned out, and Margaret found Roger in George's mouth often, actually daily. She finally realized that George was not going to hurt Roger. He actually carried him very tenderly in his mouth. This seemed most unusual. Why did George not treat this little hamster the way he did all his bugs, birds and poor innocent Fred? She snapped a photo and sent it to Anna when one day she found Roger asleep on top of George. Anna was concerned at first, but Margaret explained that the two had a very unlikely friendship. Somewhat similar to what she and Anna had, interestingly enough.

Four months into sharing a house with Anna, Anna started seeing someone. It was inevitable but Margaret had still hoped it wouldn't happen. She quickly implemented a 'No Men in My G-Rated House Rule', which Anna didn't like but respected. Probably because she knew that Margaret had a security camera at both her front and back door. It changed their relationship, mostly because Margaret thought they were moving too fast and Anna seemed a bit desperate to meet someone. She wasn't sure she approved of this boy who only seemed to invite Anna out when it was convenient for him. He did live an hour away and that made things difficult, but Margaret felt protective of Anna and a bit responsible. Though she was an adult, she felt like one of Margaret's children. Margaret tried to tell her what she would tell her own kids in this situation. There was no hurry. Take it slow. Make sure that he is who he appears to be. It's easy to put on appearances, especially when you don't live in the same town.

Despite all the late-night talks and advice, six months in, Anna told Margaret that she was pregnant. They talked for hours about Anna's options. Anna was stronger than Margaret had ever seen her, dead set on raising this baby. Margaret offered her encouragement, saying she would be there for her, but was so relieved when Anna's parents welcomed her back home. She wanted the best for Anna and was thankful to know she had the support of her family. The day she moved out, Margaret felt a combination of relief and sadness. She was grateful for her time with Anna, but she resolved to not offer her home up to any more students.

Margaret did notice a pattern that many young people were wanting to learn a second language. This gave her hope for the future. One of her favourite, but most exhausting students, was a young man named Paul. He had a particularly unique way of butchering the beautiful French language. He just ploughed in, no fear at all. While normally this would be admirable and encouraged, Paul just didn't bother to conjugate any verbs, nor did the subject necessarily fit with the verb. It was incredibly hard to follow him. An outsider might think he was fluent, the way he spoke French at a rapid pace with hardly a breath between sentences. What Paul possessed was obviously an extensive vocabulary with no grammar whatsoever. He shared that he had lived in Martinique for a year, so he had picked up this hodge-podge French that really made very little sense. Just lots of words strung together that were not cohesive at all.

It did not help that Paul was always hyped up on caffeine. He admitted that he usually added eight shots of espresso to his coffee to wake up in the morning. If Paul were any more awake, he might be dead. He physically had to hold onto the table to keep himself still. Yet, he was endearing.

Claire said Margaret found everyone to be endearing. This was not true of course, but she did really care for her students and found herself mothering each one. She told Paul, just as a suggestion, that he might feel better if he only put in, say, four shots of espresso, instead of eight.

Her students were amused by her too, she could tell. She wondered what they really thought of her. She hoped it was more quirky, nerdy middle-aged lady instead of weird and in your business old lady. Well, surely it was a good sign that they stayed with her.

Months turned into years, and the number of students grew. Joseph and Claire told her that she was doing too much, so she found herself hiding some of her students. She loved her time with them, and as long as it didn't interfere with her studies or her family, she didn't see the problem. Her children were living on their own, and she could not spend her time just waiting for them to come home.

Joseph did put his foot down when he found out Margaret had been mentoring a child for several years. Patricia volunteered with a non-profit and begged Margaret to sign on as a mentor. Her son was all for the mentoring, but he could not believe she drove into this child's inner-city neighbourhood to pick her up weekly for a couple hours of ice skating or a movie or perhaps just a walk so they could talk. Margaret blew it by telling Joseph that the child's mom was obviously on drugs, since she could not string together a sentence and barely lifted her head from the sofa when Margaret picked up the little girl. The sweet child had told her the family spent many nights on the floor because of gunshots in the neighbourhood. It shattered her heart.

"Can't you just meet her at the centre like all the other mentors?" Joseph had asked her. Margaret knew that would be the logical answer, but what if the little girl couldn't get there? Margaret's guilt always got the best of her, but after a few months of negotiation Joseph put his foot down, forbidding her to go back to that house. She was so grateful she had a son who loved her enough to take care of her and she felt for the first time the roles might be reversing ever so slightly and now it was her children telling her to 'make wise decisions' instead of the other way around. While Margaret agreed with her son and vowed to meet her sweet mentee only at the centre, she still secretly visited the little girl's house from time — to-time. He didn't need to know everything.

Chapter 12

Margaret had gone on exactly three first dates since her divorce. Three too many, if you asked her. She went several years without anyone prying, but eventually, her grace period ended and her friends started pushing her to get back out there.

The first was a set-up from her old college friend, Beth. The man was a doctor who Beth occasionally worked with as a physician's assistant.

"So, here's the scoop," she said one spring afternoon while they were out for a walk. "Apparently, he got divorced last year. One kid, full head of hair, and a house in the Hamptons."

Margaret rolled her eyes. "Great. Anything about, I don't know, his personality? Or interests?"

"I don't know him all that well, but he's very respected and incredibly smart. Plus, there's a great smile that goes with that head of hair," she said, nudging Margaret.

"You're not going to let me off the hook, are you?" Margaret asked.

"Nope."

The doctor made reservations at the nicest steakhouse in town. It was the kind of place Margaret dreaded going. She preferred cosy over stuffy.

Margaret spotted him right away. Beth was right, he was very handsome. But what Margaret noticed was the way he was speaking to the waiter.

"This isn't what I ordered," he was saying, pointing at a bottle of red wine. "This is the 2017. I clearly asked for the 2012."

The waiter rushed off apologetically.

Oh geez, Margaret thought. It made her skin crawl to witness such blatant rudeness. She would have hightailed it out of there — he hadn't even noticed her yet — if she didn't think Beth would be furious at her for standing him up.

Instead, she smiled and introduced herself, trying to shake off that first impression.

What followed was a dinner that lasted way too long, with the doctor gabbing nonstop about his accomplishments, his cars, his wine collection, barely asking Margaret anything beyond her name.

Margaret was historically terrified of blind dates because she imagined long, awkward silences that she would inevitably fill with some idiotic comment about an article she had read about cheesemaking or something. But that situation didn't sound half bad now. With this man, she felt completely invisible.

She thanked him half-heartedly for dinner, rushing home to the comfort of her home. She sank into a hot bath and closed her eyes, hearing George's gentle purr on the rug next to her.

Why, she wondered, would she want to waste any of her precious time having dinner with a jerk when she was already perfectly content at home? Society seemed to pity the image of a woman of a certain age home alone with her cat, but Margaret couldn't think of anything better. She didn't feel like she needed a relationship to be happy, but everyone else in her life had a hard time accepting that fact.

Inevitably, it wasn't long before Margaret was conned into attending another much-dreaded blind date. This time the dreaded affair was set-up by Rachel. She showed up to their coffee date one morning bursting with excitement.

"Oh my gosh, I met the *best* guy for you at a bookstore yesterday!" Rachel squealed.

"Raaach," Margaret moaned.

"I know, I know, but he was darling and seemed really interested in you," Rachel replied.

"What were *you* doing in a bookstore?" Margaret joked, hoping to change the subject.

"Don't be a jerk," Rachel said playfully.

Margaret raised her eyebrows.

"Okay, fine, I was buying a gift for my mother-in-law. But that's beside the point."

Margaret could tell she wasn't going to get out of this, so she sat back and sipped her coffee while Rachel gushed.

"Anyways, like I said, he's precious, and he wants to take you to dinner this weekend!"

"All right," Margaret said with a sigh, "I surrender. Just tell me when and where."

Rachel clapped her hands like an excited child, and Margaret couldn't help but smile despite her feeling of dread towards yet another blind date.

She arrived at the restaurant five minutes late. It literally pained her to be tardy, but not nearly as much as the thought of sitting alone at a table waiting for her date to arrive.

Margaret scanned the restaurant once, and her stomach dropped thinking that she might still have beat him there. Everyone inside was in pairs or groups, except for an older man sipping a glass of wine.

She glanced right passed him initially, but then their eyes met, and he cocked his head and waved. Margaret smiled. It was Tom, the owner of her favourite local book shop. Even though she hated running into acquaintances, she figured it would be impolite to not say hello, so she headed over.

Suddenly, mid-walk, it dawned on her.

Ohshitohshitohshit, was all she could think as she walked slowly to the table.

"Hi, Tom," Margaret began nervously. "You're not, by chance, waiting on a date, are you?"

"Oh boy," he said chuckling, "is it obvious?"

"No, not at all," she replied quickly. "It's just... I'm also here to meet a date. Someone my friend met in a bookshop, believe it or not." She shrugged sheepishly. She could feel her cheeks flushing.

Tom tilted his head back and laughed warmly. Margaret was relieved by his good humour. She herself felt mortified.

"I'm sorry, Margaret," he said, throwing his hands in the air. "Your friend didn't tell me your name."

"Gosh, yeah," Margaret said, "she didn't tell me your name either." She let out a little laugh.

"Listen, I'd be honoured to have a date with you," Tom said slowly, "but I think we can both agree that I'm a little bit old for you."

Margaret tried to think of a kind reply, but thankfully he beat her to it.

"What do you say I buy you dinner nonetheless? Just as friends. There's actually a new book I ordered for the shop that I'd love to discuss with you." He gestured towards the empty seat across from him.

Margaret figured there was no polite way out of this, plus she was starving, so she took a seat.

She ordered a glass of wine, and asked Tom about the book he'd been reading while he was waiting. He cheerfully discussed the stack of novels he was currently tackling, and told her he thought she might enjoy a new novel out, *American Dirt*. The bookstore actually had the author coming for a signing and she would discuss a bit about the book if Margaret wanted to come. He also caught her up on the latest happenings at the shop and his excitement over his upcoming trip to

Scotland where he would play golf and drink scotch with his grown son. He beamed as he talked about waiting his whole life for this experience.

They sat for two hours discussing beloved books and favourite authors. When they got up to leave, Margaret gave Tom a hug and thanked him for a delicious dinner. She told him she'd see him soon at the shop, and they went their separate ways.

She no longer felt embarrassed; she and Tom had shared a good laugh about the situation and she actually had quite enjoyed herself. Still, Margaret could have *killed* Rachel for this. Tom was, what, sixty-five years old?

Back at home, Margaret called Rachel from bed.

"Hi! How was it? Did you love him?"

"Yeah, he's great," Margaret began. "I won't even get in to the fact that you set me up with someone my dad's age without even warning me, but why in the hell did you not tell me he *owned* the bookstore where you met him?"

"Um…" Rachel paused.

"Did you seriously think I wouldn't know the owner of the only local bookstore in town? I've known Tom for years. I'm a member of his book of the month club, for crying out loud!"

Rachel was silent for a moment, but soon Margaret heard her tell-tale snort.

"I'm so sorry, Marge, really," Rachel said through fits of laughter. "I seriously didn't even consider it. I… I just thought he'd be so perfect for you."

Margaret wanted to be annoyed, but the more Rachel laughed, the more she had to fight laughter herself.

"I also thought he looked really good for his age," Rachel squeaked out. Margaret could tell she was laughing so hard she was crying.

Finally, Margaret couldn't help it any more, and she began to laugh so hard that tears streamed down her face.

When they both calmed down, and Rachel had apologized profusely for this faux-pas, Margaret made one firm request, no more set ups.

Chapter 13

Early the following year, Margaret was enjoying a quiet morning as a soft snow fell outside her window. Her spring semester was set to begin in two weeks, and she was scanning through her books to make sure she was prepared. Naturally, she had already purchased her books and a fresh spiral notebook before the holidays, but she liked to have everything set out and organized just-so before the first day.

She heard her phone ringing in the kitchen, and when she picked it up, she heard an unusually cheerful Jill on the other line.

"Hello, you!" Jill chirped.

"Hi, yourself," Margaret said, taking a sip of her coffee.

"I'm going to get straight to the punch here, Marge — I have a guy that you really, truly *have* to meet."

"Come ooooon," Margaret groaned.

"Look, I know you said the doctor was a disaster, but this is different."

"And how's that?" Margaret demanded.

"He's Mark's friend from work. So, actually, it's not me setting you up, it's Mark. And you know he's way nicer than me," Jill rambled quickly.

"True," Margaret replied sarcastically.

Mark was Jill's husband, and he was, genuinely, one of the nicest guys, Margaret knew. He was the calming force to Jill's fiery personality, and Margaret had always admired their relationship.

"I just texted you a picture, check it out," Jill continued.

Margaret pulled up her text and took a look at the headshot Jill had sent.

"Cute," she admitted, "but so was Doctor Asshole."

"Gross," Jill said with a giggle. "But seriously, Margaret," she continued, "Mark has been talking about how great this guy would be for you for months. Just have one drink with him, please."

Margaret begrudgingly met Michael two weeks later at a little pizza place she and her family had always loved. She had to admit that she liked that he suggested this place instead of something fancy and stiff. She felt comfortable here.

Since Jill had shown her a picture of Michael, Margaret could at least avoid the painful act of asking strange men if they were her date, only to be tapped on the shoulder by their irritated wives returning from the bathroom.

He was sitting at the bar laughing with the bartender. He appeared friendly and warm, so Margaret reminded herself as she walked over to keep an open mind.

He smiled upon seeing her, hopping up and giving her a big hug. Margaret was always taken aback when people went in for a hug rather than a handshake. She hugged her children and her parents, and occasionally her close friends (not by choice), but she found it bizarre that there were people who were audacious enough to hug complete strangers.

She tried to shake off this overly-intimate act as she took a seat at the bar.

"What can I grab you to drink?" the bartender asked.

"Umm," she stammered, "how about just a glass of Cab?"

She could feel Michael looking at her, and for some reason it made her feel flustered. He was even more attractive in person. That, combined with his warm and outgoing nature, made her stomach do somersaults.

If he noticed, which surely, he did, Michael didn't let on a bit. He jumped right in to asking Margaret about her French classes, which was a topic she was excited to discuss. She was taking French phonetics and loving every minute of it. Reading the French phonetic alphabet took every bit of her concentration, and when she studied, she fell into that perfect state of flow, where hours can seem like mere minutes. Suddenly she realized she had been rambling on about French dialects and what she had learned the previous semester about Charlemagne, the first king of France.

"Gosh," Margaret said, taking a deep breath, "I'm so sorry, I don't usually talk this much." She must have been boring him to death.

Michael smiled revealing one adorable dimple on his perfect five o'clock shadow of a face.

"I like listening to you talk," he replied earnestly. "It's fantastic you've found something you're so passionate about."

Michael was easy to talk to, and when she finally gave him the chance, had plenty of interesting stories himself to add to the conversation. Like her, he was divorced, and he had one child, a daughter who was in high school. His eyes lit up when he mentioned her, which made Margaret like him even more.

The evening was easy and enjoyable, and when they stepped outside into the chilly night to say their goodbyes, he leaned in close to her, tucked her hair gently behind her ear, and softly kissed her cheek. He lingered just long enough for her to close her eyes and inhale. He smelled clean and his body was warm up against hers. Margaret still didn't *want* to date, but this was the first time in a long time she had that buzzy feeling she got when she liked someone.

Her phone buzzed as she pulled into her driveway. 'Enchanté, Margaret!' the text from Michael read. She smiled, feeling like a teenager with a crush.

Chapter 14

After one month of dating, Margaret finally let Michael sleep over at her house. She had wanted to keep things casual, and was nervous about letting him into her space in that way.

When she awoke at six-thirty, she was surprised to see that he was already up. She could hear him puttering around in the kitchen, and she quickly reached for her robe. It felt strange to have a man in her house, making coffee while she lay in bed.

She walked sleepily into the kitchen and was met with instant chatter.

"So, I was thinking, we could go for a walk this morning, then Sarah's got a soccer game, which obviously you don't have to go to if you don't want, but then maybe we could meet back up for dinner?"

He was talking a million miles per hour. Margaret looked longingly at the coffee maker.

"Oh, sorry," he laughed, handing her a mug. "Good morning, by the way." He gave her a soft kiss on the head.

His was the kind of energy she could never understand. She took a sip of the hot coffee and contemplated the day he had laid out before her. It sounded perfectly lovely, but all she really wanted to do was spend the day alone, reading and tidying up the house that she'd neglected the past few weeks during her newfound romance.

"You know," she began, "I'm actually feeling really wiped out. Rain check?"

Michael looked disappointed, but quickly put a smile on his face. "Yeah, of course. Are you okay?"

"Just tired," she fibbed. She felt fine physically, but was beginning to experience the more abstract exhaustion that comes along with constant social interaction. She and Michael had spent quite a bit of time together in the last month, and she was missing her time alone.

"I'm gonna head home and hop in the shower," he said, interrupting her train of thought. "Call me if you need anything!"

She felt slightly guilty. She had come to understand that, unlike her, Michael was the kind of man who could spend all of his time around people.

"Sorry to miss out!" she shouted as he was leaving. He winked sweetly and hopped into his car. Margaret watched him drive off and felt the familiar excitement of anticipating an entirely free day. She was, in fact, the opposite of sorry to miss out. She inhaled the silence and immediately felt calmer. Some people gained energy by being around others, but Margaret gained energy with time alone. She loved people, very much.

But if she didn't get enough time alone, she started to feel depleted and anxious.

Margaret decided she'd start the day by making herself eggs, always scrambled and with a piece of toast from the best bakery in town, and working on her French paper that was due next week. She'd been slacking in her studies, and hated the feeling of being behind. She loved studying, but the papers kind of hung over her head. Of course, starting was always the hardest part. Once she started writing, there was no stopping her. So she cozied up in her small office that doubled as a guest room, and dove into her research.

Margaret had finally made her way into the heart of her French studies, and was now enrolled in early French history. She'd always thought of herself as a history nerd, but she was both stunned and thrilled to discover that there was still so much to learn. She couldn't believe that she really didn't know much about the French Revolution, about why it had occurred. That the people were fed up with the monarchy and fed up with being hungry. That they had stormed the Bastille and freed the prisoners and armed them and actually overthrown the king. It was really quite amazing. The king at that time, King Louis the XVI, had luxuriated at Versailles while his people starved and they were over it. Little did the monarchs know that their life was soon to come to an end. The people had had it. And then there was King Charlemagne. Her mom told her that they were in some way related. And she insisted that any family member that went to Paris must have their photo taken with his statue. Of course, Margaret had listened politely, but had only heard yada, yada, after a certain point, and now, thanks to her disinterest, she had no idea how they were related. One day her parents would be gone, and she would regret every time she had not paid more attention to them. The stories would be gone with them. Margaret pushed that thought aside. Luckily for everyone, the statue was next to Notre-Dame, so it wasn't much of an imposition. Someday when she made her way back to France, she'd take the damn photo yet again. But Charlemagne really was something else. He saved France from the Barbarian invasions and the pope crowned him emperor. And even though he was illiterate, he believed strongly in an education and helped to set up schools.

In addition to the Charlemagne photo, Margaret's mom insisted on a beret from Paris anytime anyone she knew went. And it had to be from the fancy department store, Galeries Lafayette. It could not be from the street corner. And woe to the relative that tried to deceive her. She checked the label. It had better say '100 percent wool' and more importantly, it had better say 'Made in France'. She plopped these on Margaret's endlessly patient father's head and he reluctantly wore them. Fortunately, a man in his seventies can look cute in a beret, even in the US, and Margaret thought he secretly knew he looked nice due to all of the comments he got. The funny thing was that no one in France wore berets.

No one. Maybe a very old gentleman in a tiny rural village somewhere, but that was it. And yet, they were sold on every street corner, in every colour, to tourists who couldn't buy enough of them. They did make a cute souvenir, Margaret had to admit.

That afternoon, eyes bleary from too much time on the computer, Margaret decided she would finally get around to touching up the paint around her house, something that needed to be done desperately thanks to her clumsiness and George's affinity for scratching.

She cracked open the paint can and started the French playlist that Claire made for her. She poured a bit of paint on to a paper plate, and carried the plate and a small paintbrush around the house, touching up nicks in the walls while humming along to the music. The windows were open, *C'est si bon* was playing; she felt utter bliss. She shared her French music with her mom, who didn't understand a word, but so loved the music. She loved sharing things with her mom. Her mom was the best listener she had ever known. Whenever Margaret talked, her mom gave her entire attention. She was utterly interested in anything Margaret was doing and kept up with everything, from what she was wearing, to what she was reading. Margaret was really fortunate to have a mother and a daughter whom she adored, and who actually adored her back. It made her want to call them both right then. These two women were her life. Well, and George, but he was not a woman.

All the while, a thought was occurring to Margaret that she had been trying to suppress for the past couple of weeks.

This isn't what I want.

She hated that she was thinking such a thing, especially about someone as wonderful as Michael. It wasn't anything he'd done or not done, it just wasn't 'it'. Her tranquillity shrunk away as she finally let this thought creep in. She was crazy not to pursue this relationship, wasn't she? All her friends would certainly think so. There wasn't a single thing wrong with him. She just didn't miss him when they weren't together, and sometimes when he was with her, she actually wished he wasn't. She needed to tell him now, before things went any further. She felt sick. He did not deserve this.

'Hey, can you swing by to chat?' She sent the text message and started nervously pacing. Almost immediately, her phone rang.

Shit. She had to answer it.

"Hi," she said quietly.

"Is everything okay?"

"Yes… and no. I was hoping to talk to you in person," she responded, trying to muster up the courage not to just blurt out *never mind bye!*

He was quiet.

"I don't want to do this over the phone."

"It's okay, Margaret. Just tell me," he said softly.

"Michael, I am so sorry, but I don't think I want to be in a relationship," she said, squeezing her eyes shut as she braced for his response.

He was silent for a moment, and then surprised her when he said, "I know."

She was trying to figure out how he could know that when he continued.

"Beth told me you weren't interested in dating, and then you told me you didn't want anything serious when we first went out. You haven't really led me on. I was just... hoping you'd change your mind."

Her heart sank the way it always did when people were kind when they easily could have been ugly. She was letting go of a good man. She wanted to cry, but the relief she felt told her this was the right decision. Margaret knew he'd find someone else, and she could only hope that whoever it was would be as great as he was. She might even be a bit jealous of the woman who found this gentle man, because he would be the kind of man who would put her first and take good care of her. But he was not for her.

"I'll always be glad I met you," he said after a long pause.

"Me too," Margaret replied. She meant it with her whole heart.

Chapter 15

One rainy late spring morning, Margaret walked into the café to meet the three older gentlemen who made up her French Group. She was feeling a little sleepy but ready as always to speak French and, to her surprise, to spend time with the most unusual but incredibly endearing group of seniors she now considered friends. Arnold was busy cleaning his teeth with his special toothpick that he, most unfortunately, pulled out all the time. He had lost the sort of filter that told one to not do such an activity in public. At the table, especially. Margaret had had her mom send her some of her dad's old berets and she relished the moment of passing them out to the men. She noticed tears in Bernard's eyes, and the others were noticeably touched. They all put them on, of course, and Margaret had the waitress take their picture. She tried to be in this moment, which she had a feeling she would treasure more someday than even now. She was glad to be here, in this place, at this time.

Margaret immediately noticed an excitement in the air, despite the dreary weather. The men were up to something, that much was obvious, and they could not seem to wait to tell her.

"Bonjour, ma belle chérie," Arnold said as Margaret pulled up a chair. Ever the feminist, Margaret would typically not put up with some man calling her 'my beautiful dear'. However, for some reason, she found herself letting it slide with these men who often reminded her of her father, and who she knew meant no offense.

"Salut, Arnold. Ca va tout le monde?"

"Oh good, good," Frank chimed in. "Apologies for the Anglais, but we've got a little proposal for you, and heaven knows it'd take us all day to say it in French."

"A proposal?" Margaret said, smiling as she sat down.

"How would you like to accompany us to Quebec for their world-famous Christmas Festival?" Frank asked, eyes glimmering.

"Well, that sounds like a wonderful idea," Margaret responded. She assumed they were speaking about next year, or the year after, and by then she could make up some excuse for not being able to go. Either that, or one of them would be too old (or worse) to travel. She quickly shook that dark thought off and smiled at the group, as she took a sip of the hot coffee they had graciously already ordered her.

The men looked at one another, seemingly pleased. "Well great," Arnold chirped. "Bernard here figured out how to get the flights pulled up on his phone, so we're booking them as we speak."

"Booking flights? Right now?" she asked as her heart started pounding. Her mind was spinning with possible excuses.

"Come on, you," Bernard said, nudging her with his elbow. "Don't let us old francophones take on Canada all by ourselves."

Margaret chewed on her lip as she tried to think. On the one hand, just imagining getting aboard an airplane practically made her break out in a nervous sweat. But on the other hand, visiting snowy Quebec during the most magical season sounded like a dream come true. It would be her first-time speaking French with actual native French speakers. She could practice all she wanted as she sipped wine and ordered pastries in darling cafés. Margaret knew she would be deeply disappointed if she missed out on this opportunity simply because of her fear. She never would have guessed that three old men would end up enticing her to hop on a flight in the midst of her phobia, and yet here she was, finding herself wanting to say yes to this bizarre yet charming offer.

"Okay, boys," she finally replied. "Count me in."

Margaret only realized what she had actually agreed to when she mentioned the upcoming trip to the girls that weekend.

"Wait, you're going to Canada... I mean, you're *flying* to Canada to spend Christmas with a bunch of old men?" Jill asked, clearly baffled, as the girls sat around Margaret's kitchen table drinking Pinot Noir. Jill was the scandalous one of the group, always getting them in trouble when they were young. Once, they had taken a trip to Las Vegas. Margaret and Rachel had shared a room, but Jill had insisted on staying on her own. They all went down to gamble. Margaret and Rachel had run out of money in an hour, but Beth was flush and she generously kept giving them tokens, which they kept losing. Eventually she and Rachel decided to head to bed, as they could see Jill was up for an all-nighter.

The next morning, they knocked on her door. They could see she had had a rough night. "You okay?" worried Margaret.

"Well, I think so," Jill said slowly. "The thing is, I woke up naked with a five-hundred-dollar chip in my hand."

"Oh my gosh," Rachel shouted. "You're a prostitute now!" They couldn't help themselves. Despite the fact that she may have in fact stolen or sold her body for the chip, they were all laughing until their stomachs ached.

Margaret had residual anxiety for Jill, who brushed it aside as they headed down to breakfast. They did make Jill go back with them that night, but Jill being Jill, they were pretty sure she snuck back out. This story came out frequently when they were drinking. Jill was the rebellious one. Rachel was the pretty one. The drop dead gorgeous one actually. People stopped her on the street to tell her how pretty she was, which was awkward for Jill and Margaret who were standing beside her. She shrugged it off gracefully. She was also very funny and loved playing jokes on her friends. Last April Fool's she had snuck into Margaret's house and put a rubber band around the spray nozzle of her faucet so that when Margaret turned the water on, it shot straight at her face. She knew who was to blame. It was constant. And Margaret was the nerdy friend that for some inexplicable reason they liked. She was thankful for their friendship. They had always been way cooler than her, but they insisted they loved her quirkiness and they thought she was hilarious. She wasn't really that funny, it's just that she was constantly messing up, which they found amusing.

Once, when Joseph was playing baseball with Jill and Rachel's sons, they were all standing around waiting for the boys to finish up. Margaret could overhear some men talking to the coach.

"Murph, you're doing a great job with the boys," one man said.

And another dad added, "Thanks, Murph, for all your hard work."

So when 'Murph' walked over to the ladies, Margaret said, "Hey, Murph, we really do appreciate all you do for us." He smiled strangely and walked away. Rachel and Jill looked at Margaret and burst out laughing.

"What?" she could feel her face turning red.

"His name is Bill Murphy. Not Murph." Beth blurted out. "Are you guys new best friends, or something?"

This should have bothered Margaret more, but it was so typical of her she almost didn't care, although she took great care to call him Mr Murphy for the rest of the season. It wasn't the first, and certainly wouldn't be the last time she made this kind of faux-pas.

Margaret began to wonder what she was thinking, booking this trip. First of all, she was flying (her worst fear) and visiting a foreign country with a group of men, one of whom was bound to die while they were there, and she was somehow excited. Scared, yes, but excited enough to go anyway. She loved having these odd men in her life. They really cared about her, and she cared about them too.

"Not actual Christmas. We're going December second, during the Christmas Festival."

"It sounds magical, Marge," Rachel chimed in with a wink. "But," she continued cautiously, "how do you feel about flying again?"

Unfortunately, they all remembered "the incident" as well as she did. Did she feel great about flying considering the last time she did she wound up with her head between her knees, wondering where she put her will? No. But she also could not imagine a life where she was trapped by her own anxieties.

As part of the deal with the men, she had said that if she was going to jet off to Quebec with them, they had to take a French cooking lesson with her. She chose macarons. Her absolute favourite cookie. The macaron is one mother of a cookie to master. The list of ingredients was easy enough — Margaret probably had everything at home — but getting the syrup at just the right temperature while simultaneously beating the eggs was just not happening for Margaret and the men. The teacher effortlessly showed them again how to do it, then set them up with a partner to give it a try.

She grabbed Arnold, the only one who would really try, and she playfully threw a bit of flour at him. He threw some back and before they knew it, they were already in trouble with the teacher. They put their aprons and their serious faces on and got to work. She set Arnold to whipping the egg whites until they reached the soft peak stage, something neither one of them had ever heard of. The teacher came by and said they could add the sugar, which Margaret was melting on the stove. Apparently, the mixture on the stove needed to be at a soft ball stage before being added to the egg/almond flour mixture that Arnold was working on. Once again, she and Arnold were snickering about the 'soft ball stage'. They needed a list of definitions. And pictures to go with it. But the instructor rushed off to assist Bernard and Frank, who had smoke billowing up from their station. In the end, their macarons were all disastrous. The instructor brought out a backup tray and they ate the cookies with gratitude. Maybe some things are better left to the professionals.

Chapter 16

The morning of the trip, Margaret followed Dr Montgomery's plan to a T, wake up, make herbal tea in lieu of coffee and then do a guided meditation. Her bags were packed and set out neatly along with her carry-on and passport. Her phone was charged, her Xanax was within arm's reach (just in case), her wallet was in her bag, and she had remembered to call the bank to let them know she would be using her credit cards in Canada. The last thing she had to do every time she flew was to call her mom to go through a completely ridiculous dialogue. Margaret always said, "Mom, promise I won't die," to which her mom would answer simply, "You won't die." Her mom knew not to offer any other advice; that was her lucky charm; just those two silly sentences helped her immensely. She was not allowed to say anything else, so they hung up.

Dr Montgomery told her that the less stress she had the morning of the flight, the better. However, it wasn't *travel* anxiety that she struggled with. That had been David's forté. He loved flying, but it was preparing for the trip that turned him into a frenzied mess. Mr Laid-Back was always a ball of nerves starting the night before a trip. He inevitably realized at eight p.m. that his

ID was about to expire or that he had forgotten to wash any of his socks and thus began a very unpleasant twelve to fourteen hours for everyone as he rummaged through drawers muttering profanities. His stress continued into the morning as he panicked that they would be late to the airport or that he forgot to pack any underwear; something that did actually happen on a very memorable trip to San Diego.

Meanwhile Margaret, who had packed a full twenty-four hours in advance, began to grow more jittery by the minute thinking not of late arrivals or forgotten undergarments, but of the flight itself. She knew what it was. She was afraid of being afraid. On the way to the airport the two of them inevitably formed what the kids jokingly called 'the perfect storm'.

"Babe, did you grab my iPad?" David would start inadvertently quizzing Margaret the entire way to the airport, as if it made a difference now. Margaret would hold it up to show him, palms sweating as she noticed on the itinerary that the aircraft they were traveling in, was a 737 instead of her preferred 747.

"But what about—"

"Charger? Got it."

"What's the deal with this traffic," he would grumble, glancing at his watch.

David's nervous blabbering would continue while Margaret closed her eyes and took shaky breaths. The kids would laugh at both of them, placing their forefingers on their thumbs chanting 'ommm'. Why weren't they as neurotic as their parents? Maybe they just hadn't had time to become that way yet. She remembered a time when she loved to fly and wished she could still feel that way. When she was young, she had felt absolutely no fear. She had loved the bumps, the bigger the better, thinking it was some kind of roller coaster ride. She had loved getting stuck in some city and having to spend the night, only to get to fly out the next morning. It had all been exciting, not scary in the least.

Of course, terrified or not, underwear remembered or not, they survived every trip. Everyone was lighter on vacation, and Margaret held tight to that feeling as she anticipated her journey to Quebec. Her family always grew closer after traveling together, and the memories grew fonder as they looked back on them now. She loved the "Remember when…" that inevitably came up over holidays and family dinners.

She had decided to share her troubles about her flight anxiety with the boys. She genuinely did not want their sympathy; she just found that when she said her fears out loud their powers diminished, at least a little bit. So when Margaret arrived at the airport, they were all there and ready to do what they could to ease her mind.

Bernard had insisted not only on paying to upgrade everyone's ticket, but to cover their admission to the Admiral's Club so that they could all "travel together in style." Bernard was very wealthy, a fact that he felt comfortable sharing often. On their first meeting, he told Margaret all about his medical career and successful start-up business which he sold, investing the proceeds and tripling his money. But what he lacked in tact, he made up in generosity. Not only was he constantly picking up the tab or gifting everyone bottles from his impressive wine collection, but Margaret learned that two years ago when Arnold's wife passed away, Bernard started sending his housekeeper over twice a week to help out.

Arnold and his wife had been together for fifty-two years and when she died, he was overwhelmed not only with grief, but with the upkeep of their large family home that he couldn't bear to sell. He spoke often of 'my Molly', which always made a lump well up in Margaret's throat, as tears inevitably welled in Arnold's eyes. She wasn't sure if he would have made the perfect husband for her if he was thirty years younger, but she thought possibly so. However, he had had one love in his life. Molly was still and always would be his constant companion. A love like that was incredibly rare. Arnold and Molly had been very lucky.

She was deeply thankful that these men had each other to lean on, and she found herself thankful that she too could rely on them, like three surrogate fathers that she never knew she needed. They sent her flowers on Valentine's Day and gave her a Christmas present during the holidays. They shared her. In return, she had them over to help decorate her Christmas tree and thought up little odd jobs that would give them an excuse to come over and to feel helpful. Of course, the jobs had to be something somewhat simple, like changing filters or lightbulbs. But, turned out, it actually was helpful to have three men around as she had no idea where the filters were in her house, what exact function they provided and where to buy them. These guys had come around at just the right time. They scolded her for dirty filters and worried over her when she refused to set her alarm. After the fiasco in her new home, when she had spent the night in her car after the alarm had gone off, she no longer set it. She would rather be killed in her bed than have that thing go off. She was sure if it did, she would have a heart attack.

Walking into the Admiral's Club, Bernard immediately flagged her down, wildly waving his arms as if she didn't notice the three old men drinking scotch at eleven a.m.

"*Bonjour, ma belle!*" There was something wonderful about being old. You could get away with most anything, like drinking heavily in the morning.

"*Bonjour, mes amis,*" Margaret replied, genuinely relieved to see them. They were so cheerful and enthusiastic that she found her nervous energy turning more to excitement. They made her take a sip of scotch and it also helped settle her.

"I do feel a little nervous to board the plane," she said as she sipped her chardonnay. Dr Montgomery told her that instead of pushing her fears down, which was her usual tactic, she should acknowledge them. Actually, lean into them. So she let herself be afraid, and she tried to welcome it, actually to invite it in. Surprise of all surprises, this seemed to help more than anything.

"I'm a bit of a nervous flyer myself," Frank chimed in. "What do you say we sit next to each other?" Margaret worried what part of his body he would show her next.

Frank seemed anything but nervous, and Margaret was able to catch a bit of his confidence. As they lined up to board, Margaret kept wiping her palms on the sides of her jeans to keep them from sweating. "Boy, am I nervous," she said, trying to laugh.

"We got this, kid," said Frank as he squeezed her clammy hand. She took a deep breath and stepped aboard.

The boys insisted on doing everything for her; carrying her bag, ordering her champagne that she insisted she did not need, asking her every few minutes if she was okay. Truthfully, she was. She squeezed her eyes shut tightly during take-off, but once they reached cruising altitude, she could feel her body relax a bit. Was it the chardonnay and first-class champagne? Was it the fact that, for once, she did not over-caffeinate herself this morning? Was it, dare she say, the company?

Frank kept up a running chatter which was actually quite effective in distracting her. On top of that, Bernard kept leaning over his seat telling her all the things they were going to do. They were staying at the famous Fairmont Le Château Frontenac, right in Quebec City. They were going to catch a Christmas concert at one of Quebec's historic churches and even go ice skating. Margaret giggled at the thought of any of them on skates. There would of course be endless shopping at the Christmas Market, and most of all, they were going to practice their French. As the plane began to descend, she couldn't help but feel proud of herself for this small yet significant accomplishment. She flew on a plane again. She didn't die. She didn't have an imaginary heart attack and cause an emergency landing. And best of all, she'd made it to a place where she could soak up the French language around every corner.

The moment they arrived at the hotel, all three men agreed that it was time for a nap. Margaret agreed to meet them in the lobby for dinner, and then bundled up and strolled out the door feeling utterly giddy. Should she grab coffee first or head straight to the bookstore? Despite her many fears, being alone was not one of them. She looked forward to dinner with the boys but certainly didn't mind that they required daily naps, allowing her the freedom to explore. She walked slowly down the charming streets of Quebec City, popping into stores and feeling exhilarated each time she had a successful interaction in French. She purchased a much-needed winter hat, a scarf for Arnold, who had mentioned he had forgotten his, and a ridiculously heavy stack of books. She might have to buy another suitcase to schlep them all home, but she couldn't resist.

When it came time for dinner, the four *amis* met in the lobby for a champagne toast. Bernard announced dramatically that he had a special pre-dinner surprise, which made Margaret feel equally excited and terrified. They stepped out into the frozen night and strolled three blocks until they reached the most picturesque ice-skating rink. It looked like it belonged in a snow globe, and Margaret suddenly felt like a child on Christmas morning. She didn't even try to contain her excitement. She had grown up ice skating, and was incredibly touched that Bernard had taken note of this fact. She assumed the men would sit this activity out, considering their age and, Bernard aside, general lack of physical abilities. But to her surprise, Arnold came back from the little admissions booth with four pairs of skates. Margaret was terrified one would go down hard and the rest of their trip would be spent at the hospital, but she fought the urge to tell them to stay on the sidelines. They were all grownups who could make their own decisions, and who was she to keep them from this magnificent experience?

They all scooted gingerly out onto the ice holding hands, and within minutes her anxieties were gone. Frank took two wobbly steps and immediately retreated to the snack cart. Arnold challenged Bernard to a race, which he thankfully declined. Margaret quickly remembered how much she loved skating, and she breezed around the rink completely forgetting the cold.

"Check it out," she shouted to the boys, feeling cocky as she skated backwards.

"Woo hoo," they all cheered, as she tilted her head back and laughed, causing her to slip and fall right on her rear end. She had such warm, thick clothing on she hardly felt a thing, and she laughed even harder as all three men tried to come to her rescue, slipping and sliding and chuckling as they attempted to lift her to her feet.

They all decided that after that adventure, they deserved to splurge on hot chocolate with real whipped cream before dinner. Margaret was pretty sure Frank had spiked it with peppermint schnapps, because they were all giggly afterward as they began their walk to the restaurant. She laughed throughout the entire dinner as each of the men spoke broken French with ridiculous confidence and loved listening as they all went around the table sharing stories about their most memorable trips. Margaret was fascinated with each of their tales of travel and adventure. It was such a simple pleasure, just sharing a meal with three people who had all led such full lives. She was certain that if she'd been younger, she wouldn't have been able to appreciate their company the way she did now.

She kept thinking about how she would love to bring her mom and Claire here for a girls' getaway. They would love the cosy atmosphere that called for endless cups of hot coffee and a good glass of red wine or two at the end of the day. Margaret wasn't convinced that she would impress them with her French. There was such a different accent here and many of the words were different. She was proud that she could understand most of what was said, but the locals had difficulty understanding her with her thick American accent. She made a mental note to really buckle down on her pronunciation when she got home. Despite some minor communication errors, she and the men agreed to speak only French when shopping and dining, although they often found themselves laughing as they bumbled along.

Towards the end of the trip, she asked the guys if they would go to Ottawa with her next year and ice skate along the Rideau Canal. All three men scoffed, asking if she was trying to get them killed.

"Honey," laughed Frank, "I think we can all agree that the three of us are officially retired."

She agreed, remembering her pure fear as she watched them feebly hobble along the rink. Perhaps they could go on one of the famous chocolate tours in France. That was more their speed. She would get Claire to agree to the Ottawa skating trip. Claire was one to always say yes to her crazy ideas.

Margaret was bursting with excitement thinking about all of the trips she had yet to take. It was the first time in years that the idea of travel elicited joy and not panic. On the flight home, her nerves were just a minor inconvenience. So much so that, when Frank fell asleep in the seat next to her, she closed her eyes peacefully and drifted off herself.

Chapter 17

While she held fast in her deep commitment to become conversational, Margaret's favourite way to study French was to read anything and everything she could get her hands on. Madame Hansen had explained to her that our brains have an incredible ability to fill in the gaps when we read, so that even if we understand only half of the words in a text, we can still grasp the general idea.

Of course, Margaret was still not ready to dive into *Les Misérables*, though she dreamed of reading it in its original French, devouring Victor Hugo's exact words rather than a translation. Nevertheless, there were still countless stories she could read, and she was constantly asking her kind professor for more recommendations. Madame Hansen had excellent resources, and sent Margaret wonderful short stories and poems to read almost weekly. She loved Victor Hugo's *Demain dès l'aube*, a beautiful but tragic and true poem about Victor Hugo losing his young daughter to a drowning accident and how he would always visit her grave because he knew she was waiting for him. It made Margaret tear up every time to hear of such unconditional love, knowing that is how it is with parents and children. She would always have to read something cheerful after reading this. However much she enjoyed everything she read, Margaret was itching to delve into a *real* French novel. Margaret was used to hard work and loved a challenge. Plus, she read aloud to George and he was picking up French faster than her.

By her sixth semester, she was finally past all of the introductory and intermediate classes, and was able to enrol in the upper-level electives of her choice. Of course, the class she had been most excited about was Modern French Literature. She had anticipated this course since the beginning of her studies, and she felt so excited to begin that she could hardly stand it. It was like joining another book club where everyone was actually forced to read and discuss the book. Yes, this may have been many students' nightmare, but it was a dream come true for Margaret.

To her surprise, the first book assigned was the children's story, *Le Petit Prince*. She remembered reading it at some point in English, and recalled that it was a sweet story, but she couldn't understand why her class wasn't reading true literature.

"Madame Hansen," Margaret started cautiously, not wishing to offend her beloved professor. "I'm... surprised that we're studying a children's book in a literature course."

"I was afraid you might be disappointed, Margaret," Madame Hansen said with a shrug. "But before you write it off, give it a shot. Neither the story nor the language, are as simple as you may think."

Margaret smiled warmly and agreed to begin her studies with an open mind, thanking her professor for the hand-me-down copies that she gave each of the five students in the class.

The book felt so light in her hands. Madame Hansen had given the students three full weeks to study the book. They were to read a certain number of pages before class and come prepared to discuss metaphors, themes, writing styles and anything else they may have noticed. After completing their studies of the novel, they would each present a short literary analysis. As soon as she got home, Margaret jumped right in. As she started reading, she was immediately humbled by the number of words she didn't know. Perhaps Madame Hansen did, in fact, know what she was doing when she assigned it. And she had forgotten how this children's book had just as much to offer for adults. It had lessons to be learned. One that particularly stuck with her was, as the little prince was visiting different planets, finding that adults were so bizarre, he was really confused by the businessman he encountered who kept counting stars.

"What do you do with these stars?" the *petit prince* asked.

"I own them," the man responded.

"What's the use of owning them?" asked the little prince.

"That will make me rich," replied the man.

"What's the use of being rich?" the confused boy asked.

"So I can buy more stars," the exasperated businessman said, dismissing the little prince. The poor child went away disappointed and disillusioned with adults, not understanding them one bit.

Well, if that didn't perfectly describe humans. Running around accumulating things. And for what purpose? Why could adults not remain childlike, a dandelion more exciting than any new purchase. Margaret wanted to remember this lesson. Remember what mattered in life. But for now, she was supposed to be working on her French, not her philosophy on life. This was *les devoirs* after all.

She took her time with the reading, highlighting unfamiliar words or phrases and underlining moments or symbolism or interesting metaphors. This story would lead to some interesting discussions in class. She knew if she ever taught French, which seemed like a long shot, she would use this book. Her professor, had been spot on.

She decided she would take her three French buddies a copy of *Le Petit Prince*. She couldn't stop thinking about the message. She now had twenty-one all-time favourite books. She would also send a copy in English to her mom. She had a feeling she would love it. And mostly she would love it because Margaret loved it. She realized that the older she got, the more she treasured her family members for exactly who they were.

Chapter 18

Margaret had always been a realist. She thought this was why she was such an anxious person, because, in reality, bad things happen all the time. Being the catastrophizer that she was, Margaret always assumed that she must be a pessimist. She hated the thought of being pessimistic. She lived her life trying to be friendly and kind to everyone, she taught her kids about the importance of positivity and good humour, and yet she couldn't imagine how it was possible to be realistic and optimistic at the same time.

Lately, however, things seemed to be shifting. One dreary afternoon, she popped into the bookstore to pick up a book she'd ordered. She'd been excited for it to come in, and figured she could spend an hour or two cozied up to one of the shop's fireplaces while she began reading.

When she walked in, Tom was speaking with a customer who was having trouble deciding between two biographies. He furrowed his brow and nodded his head, listening intently. Margaret smiled thinking about the 'date' they had shared. He was such a gentleman, and had not once brought it up again, instead treating her warmly and politely as he always had.

"Margaret!" he said enthusiastically upon seeing her. "It's fantastic," he exclaimed.

She knew immediately that he was talking about the novel she had ordered. He was the only person she had ever met who went through books faster than she did.

"How on earth did you already finish it?" she asked, genuinely impressed. "Didn't they just come in two days ago?"

"I just couldn't put it down." He shrugged sheepishly, walking behind the counter to fetch her copy.

She thanked him and promised to give him a thorough review of the book once she had finished it. She walked slowly through the store, admiring each thoughtfully curated section as she scoured for the perfect reading nook. Tom had indulged her by adding a small section of foreign books. He had let her give him a list and he had graciously ordered them all. She would have to tell him to order *Le Petit Prince*. There was a comfy leather chair by a big fireplace, and she would claim it soon.

It was clear that Tom had poured his heart and soul into this store. She imagined him organizing and reorganizing each bookshelf by genre and picking out pieces of art that felt just right for the space. He was always tidying, but not in a way that made the customer feel like they couldn't get comfortable, more so in the way that someone mindfully tends to their garden.

It was interesting to Margaret that she had never considered working in Tom's bookstore. It really should be her dream job. She would get to read all the advance copies, free of charge. She could advise people on the book that was just right for them. She would enjoy that, wouldn't she? She was sure Tom would give her the job if she asked. But, thinking it over, she fretted that working here might ruin the enjoyment of coming and going as she pleased. It might turn into a 'job' and not 'pleasure'. And come to think of it, why had she never entertained the idea of dating Tom, even though he was a lot older than her? Many people married someone fifteen or twenty years older than them. If she considered it, he was ideal. They liked the same things. They were both passionate about books and travel. They both enjoyed being with people but needed time alone to read and recharge. He was handsome too, for an older man. His hair had greyed nicely, and he had sparkly blue eyes that were so sincere, and when he talked to you, he stared right into your eyes. None of that, eyes darting about business, that made her squirm. He was kind and considerate and hard working. But dadgummit, she wasn't attracted to him and she didn't think he was attracted to her either. She wondered if she spent more time on it, if friendship would turn to something more. But no way was she going to risk losing Tom as a friend, and worse, have to stop visiting the bookstore. She laughed to herself when she realized she was more worried about losing the bookstore if things ended poorly. This was the best one in town, and she came at least once a week.

Margaret tried to take her time today and really appreciate this arrangement of books that was before her. As she scanned the store, a tiny framed drawing caught her eye. It was hanging above one of the fireplaces, next to an abstract oil painting of a woman playing the violin. Margaret moved closer so she could examine the details. It was a simple sketch of a stack of books. Each book was outlined in charcoal pencil, then carefully blotted with a different shade of muted watercolour. Margaret found herself mesmerized by the unpretentious beauty of the work.

"I've got to start paying more attention to things," she said to herself, standing there in awe. It made her sad to think that she had walked by this piece of art, ignoring it for years. But perhaps she wouldn't have been so struck by it in years past. Maybe it was meant for her today.

"I picked it up at one of the Bouquinistes along the Seine," Tom said quietly, seemingly reading her mind. "The moment I saw it, I knew I needed it hanging in my shop."

Margaret smiled gratefully. "Lately," she began, "all of these signs are jumping out at me."

"Do you think it's possible that they've been there all along, but you're only just now paying attention?" Tom chided her gently. Wise man. She vowed to keep her eyes and ears open, as well as her heart.

She found 'her chair', settled in comfortably with a copy of *The Book Thief*, which Claire had told her she *had* to read, and fully immersed herself in the story, which gently melted her troubles away like butter left sitting on the counter.

Partie Trois
Le professeur

Chapter 19

Towards the end of Margaret's final French course, Madame Hansen asked her if she could stay a few minutes late to chat after class.

"Can you believe you're graduating in a few weeks?" Madame Hansen asked?

"No," laughed Margaret, "I really can't. I didn't keep track of the classes, I just kept taking them semester after semester. If you hadn't told me that I had enough credits to graduate, I would have been here again next semester."

Madame Hansen smiled affectionately. "Well, as much as we would love to have you back, it's time for you to fly."

"What am I going to do with myself?" Margaret teased.

She wasn't expecting an answer, but to her surprise, Madame Hansen chimed in. "Well, that's actually what I'd like to discuss with you."

Margaret raised her eyebrows in both surprise and hopeful interest.

"Our department is growing," Madame Hansen continued, "and I think you would make a wonderful professor."

Professor. Margaret allowed the word to really sink in. It was a dream come true.

"Well," Madame Hansen inquired politely, "what do you think?"

This time, Margaret didn't hesitate.

"Yes!"

She was so excited that she could have kissed Madame Hansen if it wouldn't get her pre-emptively fired.

"Excellent," Madame Hansen replied with a smile. "Welcome aboard, Professor James."

Just two months later, Margaret found herself back at the university, but this time she was pulling into the faculty parking lot. She had a faculty parking sticker that she did not have to pay for. She had an office, well a tiny closet, with a key just for her. People were calling her professor. She had office hours. This was real. She had still bought a new notebook with dividers with pockets. She had still bought a new outfit with Claire's help and she was still early to class. She was so excited to begin teaching that she arrived a full hour before her class was set to begin. She turned the heavy brass key that her department secretary had given her and felt the door click open. The room was dark and quiet, filled with that musty smell that had become familiar. She had, in fact, taken three of her courses in this exact room, but while the smell was the same, it felt completely different entering as a professor. Soon, there would be fourteen students seated in these desks, and now she would be the one behind the podium. She took a dry erase marker and wrote *'Bonjour, je m'appelle Madame James* on the board.

She said a silent prayer that there would be at least one student who was excited to be there, who loved French the way that she did. If that was too much to ask, she hoped, at least, that she didn't make a fool out of herself. She pushed the thought out of her head quickly, remembering what she had discussed with Dr Montgomery. *I deserve to be here*, she repeated silently.

About a week before beginning, Margaret had begun to panic that she might, in fact, be a complete fraud. What if a student asked how long she'd been teaching? Or if she'd been speaking French since she was a child? Or, worst of all, how long had she lived in France? Because any self-respecting French professor has surely lived abroad. Did her trip to Canada with the old man club count, she wondered. Or perhaps her travels with Claire were lengthy enough to count?

She thought about how she could answer these questions without telling full-blown lies.

"I have loved French language and culture my whole life!"

True.

"I have been studying French for decades!"

True, if you counted her 'French Word of the Day' app.

Dr Montgomery explained that many people, particularly women, experienced 'imposter syndrome' in their careers.

"Do you remember when you first began your career as an attorney?"

How could she forget? She had been utterly terrified of screwing something up. She felt completely unqualified and was certain that she would be fired, or at least sued, at any moment.

Those feelings never truly went away, but she settled in, worked hard, and her confidence began to grow.

David, on the other hand, never questioned his capabilities. Yes, he was slightly smarter than her, but in most ways, they were complete equals. They were both excellent attorneys, and yet he seemed to climb the corporate ladder at warp speed, while Margaret often felt stagnant.

It had been the source of a big fight one evening, when she was feeling totally defeated and self-pitying.

"I just can't believe we still live in such a sexist society!" Margaret boomed, angrily loading the dishwasher while David wiped down the table after dinner.

"Be more specific," David said nonchalantly. He clearly hadn't been listening to her story about her boss choosing a less-qualified male colleague over her for a really exciting project.

"My god, you are infuriating," Margaret said, her pulse beginning to rise. "I just got through telling you *specifically* how I was passed over, once again, by a man at work, and you weren't even listening."

He looked up from the table now. "What?"

"Are you kidding me? I work my ass off at home," she said, letting go of the plate she was scrubbing with a loud clunk. "I work my ass off at work. And nobody cares because I'm a woman."

David was just looking at her, seemingly surprised by this outburst.

"Meanwhile, you fly to the top of the pack at your job even though you golf every Friday and forget to answer emails, but it doesn't matter because you're a *man*."

David let out a deep breath, clearly frustrated. "You've been complaining for the last six months about your job, sorry I missed yet another pity party," he said, heading for the stairs. He turned back around before he left. "And I am successful at my job because I'm good at it. I speak up, I ask for opportunities, and I don't complain when they aren't just handed to me." He walked upstairs and quietly shut the door.

Margaret remembered that evening with a much softer heart now. Attacking David because sexism still existed in the workplace wouldn't get her anywhere. And questioning his own success was just plain cruel. As much as she refused to admit it at the time, he was right — she shared all of her brilliant ideas with him at home, and then completely lost her confidence in every meeting, keeping her thoughts to herself and watching her colleagues surpass her.

She was deep in thought when Dr Montgomery spoke up again. "Sometimes you just have to trust that you are qualified and deserving of your role, whether you feel it or not," she suggested. "You value your boss's opinion, right?" Dr Montgomery continued.

"Of course," Margaret quickly replied. Madame Hansen was kind and patient as a teacher, but she was also brilliant; she had studied at the Sorbonne in Paris before receiving her PHD at Yale and becoming a full-time professor. Margaret was awestruck that someone so young had already accomplished so much.

"Do you think she would hire you to teach in her program if she didn't think you were qualified?"

This thought had legitimately never crossed Margaret's mind. In questioning her worth as a professor, she was inadvertently questioning Madame Hansen's decision to hire her in the first place.

Dr Montgomery could see her mulling this over in her head. "Enjoy your accomplishment, Margaret," she said. "You deserve to be here."

So this is what Margaret told herself as she picked up the pen again and wrote the date, neatly in French, *C'est lundi, le dix-sept janvier.*

As the students began to pile in, she quickly realized that they were more nervous than she was. She let them sit wherever they wanted, and always found it interesting who picked the front row and who picked the back row. She had always been told that on average, those who sit in front do best. But do they do best because they sit in front, or do they sit in front because they are already good students and want to be as close as possible to the teacher and the blackboard? Vicious cycle, perhaps.

She enjoyed seeing who came in. She had already received their names and a small photo of each, but they looked different in person. They still had on the college student uniform of athletic shorts or leggings with baggy tee shirts and tennis shoes, their hair looking like they had just rolled out of bed. That had not changed during the last five years. There was a mix of females and males and she was so pleased to have two adult students in her first class. One woman looked to be about the age she was when she first started, maybe slightly younger, and the other, also a woman, was probably somewhere in her fifties. She imagined she had looked somewhat like them. A bit uncomfortable to be surrounded by so many young people. A bit embarrassed to look different from everyone else. She really had to hand it to them. They obviously were willing to set aside 'uncomfortable' for something they valued and really wanted. She applauded them for their courage. She remembered the feeling of stepping into the unknown; the fear of struggling, of humiliating herself, even failing. She immediately empathized with each one of her students, and decided she would be the kind of professor who didn't embarrass anyone, but encouraged them instead. If they didn't *love* French, they were, at least, not going to hate it. Not because of her.

She pushed her shoulders back and smiled confidently, greeting each student with a warm *bonjour*. A few days earlier, she had bought enough French pencils for each student. She was teaching two introductory French classes this semester, with a total of twenty-seven students enrolled. Now that the first day was actually here, she felt a little silly for buying pencils for twenty-seven adults. But the pencils were funny. They said '*Ne touche pas mon crayon*', which meant, 'Don't touch my pencil'. She was hoping it would get a laugh and not fall flat. But seeing their nervous faces, she decided it might be just the right gesture.

She introduced herself. "*Je m'appelle Madame James*," and then asked each student to do the same. They went around the room, *je m'appelle, je m'appelle*, over and over again. Margaret was trying to memorize their names as they went, but it was going to take a couple days. She was saving a funny clip from *Friends*, called *Joey learns French*, to show them in a couple days, when they had all said *je m'appelle* a hundred times already. Joey never gets the hang of it and she hoped they would think it is as funny as she did.

As they bravely spoke their first words of French, she would walk over and pass them their little prize. They were childish and cost less than a dollar each, and yet each student seemed genuinely pleased when they received their small welcome gift. That first day, Margaret decided she didn't mind being the cheesy instructor who passed out pencils if it meant making the students feel welcome. At the end of the first class, she could feel that the students had relaxed. Some even seemed to enjoy themselves. She was not about to be the teacher who stood at the front and lectured or the type that just had the students do exercises all class. No way. She wanted everyone engaged. She had decided early on to use all the strategies that she had enjoyed and learned best from when she was in school. So, she gave a very short lecture on the grammar of the day, followed by the students repeating some new words to work on their pronunciation. She passed out slips of paper so they could ask questions back and forth to a partner, then the class had a play they would read where everyone had a part. She typed the play up herself to fit with what they were learning.

Margaret also liked to include a few minutes of culture. The students seemed to really enjoy this. The first day, she had the students talk about what they assumed the French people thought of Americans and what they thought the Americans thought of the French. She reminded the class that these were just stereotypes, not necessarily true. They all shouted out things like, the French people think Americans are fat; they think we dress poorly; they think we work too hard; they think we are rude.

"And what do you think Americans think of the French people she asked?"

"They are consumed with fashion," they said, and "their children are well-behaved." She waited for someone to say that the French people are rude, and as predicted someone did. This gave her the chance to explain that sometimes these stereotypes are not correct, it is just that each country has a different culture and they have misunderstood each other.

"For example," she explained, "the Americans think that the French are rude because when an American passes a French person on the street, the American smiles and perhaps even gives a little wave and a hello. When they are only met with a stare, the Americans jump to the conclusion that the French are rude. Well, French people find it odd that Americans are over-friendly. They don't understand it. 'They don't even know us,' they say to each other. So, they find this behaviour some-what fake and most unusual. They don't know how to respond.

"Now, why do the French find the Americans to be rude? Well, in France when you walk into a shop or store, any shop or store, you say *bonjour*," she shared with her class. "It is important and it is done by every French person every single time. This came about because long ago you were walking into someone's home. The shopkeepers usually slept in the back or upstairs and so it was very polite to say *bonjour* to acknowledge an appreciation for being in a part of their home. Americans don't do this typically. If we happen to catch the shopkeeper's eye, we might say hi, but we don't feel that we have to. The French find this frightfully impolite and thus have declared Americans 'rude and impertinent'." She explained that cultural mistakes like this happen all the time and that is one of many reasons to learn another language. "It opens the mind to other cultures and helps to make one less quick to judge and more compassionate to others."

Culture time was a big hit because they could just chat and feel like they were getting out of a bit of work. Suddenly they had a lot to say. She also loved giving them a *mot du jour* (word of the day) each day. In the fall, she had decided that she would concentrate on words having to do with the home, until the holidays when they would add words like *la citrouille* (pumpkin) and *le hibou* (owl). In the spring, they would concentrate on nature and the outdoors. She couldn't wait to share the darling names for bugs in French, like she'd done with George. How do you beat the word *sauterelle* for a grasshopper or *luciole* for a lightning bug? she wondered.

Of course, it was not all sugarplums and butterflies. She knew students were staring at their phones when they looked down at their laps. She had banned phones, but she let these little slights go. But every once in a while, a student would defiantly hold their phone up and scroll, yawning, obviously bored with class. She never singled a student out, but it was always clear when she would say, "Remember that phones are not allowed in class. If I see you with your phone, you are absent today and will also receive no participation points."

She would get a scowl from the worst of them, or a red face from an embarrassed one, but it worked. Some students just didn't come, or just dropped in occasionally. They were always shocked when they had a bad grade at midterm. Most, however, were respectful and engaged.

She especially loved working with adults. No helicopter parents emailing her every day wondering why little Johnnie had not made an A, which Margaret found incredibly inappropriate. No discipline problems either, which made her sweat with discomfort. The adults had carefully chosen this class, no one had made them, and they were paying for it, so most of them really wanted to be here. Sure, many students were required by their majors to take a foreign language, but they could have taken Spanish or German.

She always made it clear that a language class is like math. It builds on itself and if you get behind, it's really hard to catch up. But these problems were minor and most days she was beaming when she left class, feeling that it had gone well and she had done her best. When the students at the end of the semester had the chance to evaluate her, she needed a tissue as she read things like, 'best teacher I ever had' and 'she really cares'. She loved sharing her passion and this just fuelled it.

Every day after class, she tidied up, grabbed her bag, and closed the classroom door, walking slowly down the hall feeling on top of the world. She liked taking the long way back to her car, enjoying her stroll through the university. There was something about being on campus that energized her. It was still warm out, but she could feel that fall was on its way in. This was going to change her life, of that, she was sure. She had a feeling she would be the type of teacher who wrote encouraging notes on their homework, putting stickers on the ones who really excelled — positive statements like *magnifique* and *fantastique*. She would think of ways to make learning more fun all day and listen to French songs to share with her class. She would bake macarons and take them to class. Actually, remembering her macaron making class, she would buy them, but still. She knew this about herself. Once she committed and loved something, she was all in. It would certainly be an adventure. One thing was certain — she absolutely loved it.

Chapter 20

After several years teaching the beginning courses, she was entrusted with a few electives. Children's Literature was a dream come true. Sharing books *in French*. She could not even stand her own happiness. It took her forever to decide which books to use. She knew the students would have to buy these books, so she would need to keep the cost down, and yet find the best classics out there. After much research and talking it over with her former professor, she decided on, *Le Petit Prince*, *Babar*, *Asterix et Obelisk*, *Martine et Bécassine* and *Le Petit Nicolas*. She started with the easiest one first, which she felt was *Bécassine*, kind of a French *Amelia Bedelia*. They all loved *petit* Nicolas, who reminded them of Dennis the Menace, a little boy who gets in all kinds of trouble. She saved her gem, *Le Petit Prince*, for the end of the semester, knowing it would leave a lasting impression. She told them to start a French bookshelf and hopefully they would add to it over the years.

Her real challenge came when she was asked to teach a French cooking class. She had always been told to never say no to an opportunity. Something along the lines of 'fake it till you make it'. She knew all about French food. She had certainly eaten enough of it and she had studied many of the most famous French chefs. She had even taken several classes, although to be fair, she had never mastered the art of the macaron. Once, she and Claire had taken a croissant class but they found it too difficult to ever try on their own. But still, she was not about to say no. She could do this, couldn't she? Well, ready or not, she agreed and committed herself to the task ahead. She had decided that they would work on one recipe a week, either in class or at home, and study one chef a week. They always started class with a short video on how to prepare the item and Margaret was listening as closely as the class, trying to remember the steps. Of course, she had practiced at home, but she had often failed and that was with no pressure. Luckily there were only five students as this was an upper division class.

She made plans for crepes to be the recipe for week one. It was almost fool proof, the ingredients were easy to bring to class and she had an electric skillet she could plug in, right in the classroom. It actually went well. Each student made their own crepe from scratch, and if they messed it up, she let them try it again, until they were confident they could do it on their own. Their assignment that week was to make a crepe at home. They would need to video their work and bring it to class to share. It turned out to be a hit. The students went all out, putting their videos to French music, and speaking in French while they cooked. They enjoyed watching each other's videos and offered one another tips and encouragement, laughing when someone completely botched their recipe but was willing to share anyway. Margaret so looked forward to hearing their stories and celebrating their triumphs. They moved on to *croque monsieur* the next week, which was basically a fancy grilled ham and cheese sandwich, but you did have to make a *bechamel* sauce. They watched a couple of videos explaining the technique; she gave them several different recipes, explaining which was easiest and sent them on their way to try this one at home. Their families and friends were beginning to love this class as they were the recipients of the fruits of their labour.

Things were going well, so Margaret got up her nerve to ask her boss if they could use the faculty kitchen to try making a soufflé. She was given several safety instructions, but they need not have worried. Margaret would check a hundred times to make sure the ovens were turned off, and would probably still not sleep that night imagining that she had not turned the dial to completely 'off'. She would worry that she forgot to wash her hands after handling the eggs and that someone might have a dairy allergy. So, safety was not something they needed to worry about with Margaret.

Unfortunately, what nobody anticipated was that the oven had not been used in years, and just as they were watching their prized soufflé rise in the oven, they began to smell smoke. Sure enough, smoke was coming out of the oven, probably from all the old grime on the bottom of it. It was possible it had never been cleaned.

Margaret grabbed a towel and tried to disperse the smoke and then promptly turned off the oven. But she made her big mistake when she opened the oven door to take out the soufflé. Smoke poured out and instantly the smoke alarm went off, followed by instructions over the intercom to evacuate the building immediately. She was mortified, but shooed the students out of the kitchen. Once in the hallway, the sprinklers turned on, dowsing everyone in a heavy-duty rainstorm. They all had to wait on the lawn, dripping wet and freezing cold, while everyone was accounted for and the firefighters came. Did they actually need to turn on their loud sirens? She thought this was a bit of overkill, but there they were all dressed for a major fire, storming into the building prepared to save lives and property. Her students were giggling, enjoying this way too much.

Her colleagues and bosses quickly forgave her and even went so far as to say it could happen to anyone. But she banned herself from the kitchen before anyone else could do it. To keep everyone safe, she had a professional chef come in to explain how to make the rest of the recipes, macarons, an easy but delicious meal of *boeuf bourguignon*, and finally they finished the semester with a *bûche de Noël*, a traditional French dessert in the form of a Yuletide log.

She had made it through, but she was suggesting Modern French Civilization for her next elective, thank you, please.

These years passed joyfully, at least most of the time. She could not imagine a life other than this one. She loved teaching as much as she had ever loved anything. And yet. And yet, there was still Paris. There was still this itch to do the one thing that she had always wanted to do. It would take more courage than she was sure she had and she would have to give up something that she adored doing.

And still, the pull strengthened.

She watched Joseph graduate from law school, so proud that he had followed in her and David's footsteps, and then find his perfect match. They had chosen to live in Boston and Margaret was so happy with their choice. It was one of her favourite cities and an easy train ride from Connecticut. His wife was lovely and very pretty. Petite. Margaret felt huge next to her. She was not at all like Margaret, which she found odd. Wasn't your son supposed to marry someone like you? Maybe this was for the best; actually, Christine was the opposite of quirky, studious and nerdy. She was practical, good with fixing things and had excellent common sense. She didn't care much for reading, which was a big flaw in Margaret's eyes. Margaret's family read. It was an integral part of who they were. She would have to fix that. Maybe the poor girl had never found the right books for her. Margaret vowed to give her a chance. She prayed with all her heart that Christine would love her son as completely and unconditionally as she had. Was that possible?

She was there when their children were born and held them in her arms, even though she was terrified, with awe. Christine chose to stay home and Margaret was proud of her for her confidence in all of her choices. First was a little boy named Henry, who looked like Joseph, but if she was honest, he pretty much looked like all babies. She was just grateful he was healthy. Margaret brought him a stack of books so they could get started right away. She also bought a stack of picture books for herself. She would read to the little munchkins when they came over. Tom had helped her pick them out. She decided while she was shopping, she might as well pick some up for one — and two-year-olds. She could see the intelligence in one week old Henry. She knew she had done many things wrong, like the time she had forgotten to pick up Joseph. In her defence, he was in high school, practically an adult, but he still talked about the traumatizing event. Or once, he had left the shower on, and it had only been noticed when the water started dripping from the ceiling downstairs, followed by chunks of plaster soon after. She had yelled at Joseph, really yelled at him, as never before, but only because she had felt that he wasn't all that sorry, and then she had gone into Claire's room and seen Claire with a pillow over her ears. She felt like an utter failure that morning with both children. She had overreacted and the guilt would remain. Forever. Oh, the joys of being a parent. Why did she remember the bad things she had done? *Focus on the good things you did*, she scolded herself. You were there for them, you played with them, you did arts and crafts with *them*. But the best thing she had done very right and could be very proud of was that she had read to her kids *every single night*.

It was her very favourite time of the day. They snuggled close, one on each side, grateful for bedtime being put off. They would let her read as long as she chose, sometimes dozing off. She read all types of books to them. Her goal was just to make book lovers out of them, and it worked. She read to them way past when they could read for themselves. Every night. When they considered themselves too old to snuggle beside her in bed, they would 'camp out' on the floor of her bedroom and she would read for a good hour. She made it until they were in their teens, when finally, she had to let go and just leave stacks of books in their bedroom. She was proud of herself for this.

Once, going to tuck Joseph in when he was about seventeen years old, almost fully grown with a beard to shave and a deep voice, she was sitting on his bed, asking him what he was reading and about his day, and Joseph blurted out, "You have way too much time for me!" She knew it was not meant as a compliment, but she loved that he had said that. She had been there for him, even if it was too often. And she had taught him to love reading and learning new things. He was a curious kid and would always love learning. A blessed one thing she did not have to feel guilty about. Henry would be a reader. She could see the curiosity in his eyes. And she would buy him lots and lots of books. And she did.

Two years later, along came little Daniel. He looked so tiny next to Henry. She was always afraid of babies. Afraid to hold them, as she was very clumsy and might drop them. Or what if she was sick, but pre-symptomatic and didn't know she was sick and she gave them something awful, like the mumps or scoliosis? Was that contagious? Who knew? She was way too afraid to take care of them. What if she forgot to feed them? What if they got hurt in her charge? No, she preferred they became sturdy toddlers before she would take care of them alone. Henry became her buddy and she loved taking him places, especially to Tom's bookstore. Both of them were happy for a good hour, searching for just the right book to buy. And in a couple of years, Daniel would be going along with them. He got a similar large stack of books, because she wanted two readers in the family. She made sure it was a wide variety, because who knew what they would love. Dinosaurs? Check. Trucks? Check. Nature? Check. Cooking? Double check. She hoped they would be a good influence on their parents.

So much advice she wanted to give her children on parenting, but she would keep imaginary duct tape on her mouth. She and David had talked about this and agreed. She vowed to nod and say, "Great idea" when they proposed outrageous ideas like letting the little tyke take swimming lessons when he was still an infant.

"Good for you," she would quip. When they tried toilet training way too early, she would simply state, "Superb decision." She really had to add a couple layers of extra duct tape when they told her there would be *no cats allowed* in their house. She could tell they would not be swayed. They did not feel like they were safe with children around. Apparently, they carried all sorts of diseases. She had so wanted to get each of the boys a kitten one Christmas.

Her own mom had loved all animals and had always let Margaret have a cat, as well as dogs, hamsters and guinea pigs. She had followed in her mom's footsteps and a wide variety of wildlife had passed through her own house. They had had iguanas, a hermit crab, turtles, dogs, cats and hamsters (which sometimes got stuck in the vents, died, and smelled for weeks). Her favourite cat growing up was named Sooner, who drooled when you petted him. He lived to be twenty-one and she was sure no cat would ever replace him. She had to call her mom when her son implemented the no cats allowed rule, who let her rant about this nonsense of cats being dangerous animals. Her mom, usually the mediator, vehemently agreed with her. Thank goodness. Her Mom still had a cat, actually a terrible cat who bit and chewed up the carpet and shredded the curtains, but she loved it and said it made the house look more lived in. Margaret agreed. A pet made a house a home. Well, she would let the little ones play with George when they came to her house. It would be their secret. And she would give them lots of candy too, because that's what grandmothers did.

Picking her grandmother's name had created quite the drama. There were several family dinners just on this topic. She had begun to hate it. Becoming a grandmother was an adjustment already, one she wasn't sure she was quite ready for, but it was happening like it or not. She had wanted to be Pooh, after Winnie the Pooh because her own grandmother had called her Pooh or Pooh Bear, knowing how much Margaret loved the books. But her daughter-in-law laughed so hard she had tears running down her cheeks.

"Our child cannot tell his friends that he's going to Pooh's house. Can you imagine the potty humour of five-year-olds?" Margaret saw her point, even if she didn't fully agree. Lucky David. Margaret had always called him Poppy when the kids were little, so he instantly had the world's cutest name.

She then suggested M, but David thought that sounded like James Bond's boss. True, but who cares? "What about Emmy?" she threw out there into the fire.

"Mom, Emmy has nothing to do with your name! No way!" Claire protested.

Since when was this her kid's decision, she thought, growing frustrated. Wasn't this going to be *her* new name? She regretted not just announcing it one evening, maybe going so far as to wear a sweater with her new name embroidered on it. But, no, she was letting them help her and it was a disaster. They didn't just dislike the names she kept suggesting, they had very strong opinions about them — they hated them! Each and every one. By the third family dinner, she threw in the towel.

"That's it" she said a bit too loudly. "I'm over it". And they knew that she was. She was close to tears. This should have been fun, and it was anything but. Why couldn't she just keep her own name. She liked her name. Why couldn't the kids just call her Margaret? This whole changing of name thing was weird and she didn't like it one bit. She tossed her napkin on the table and retreated to the kitchen.

She could hear them talking softly, probably saying things like, "Mom's so weird," or "Why is Mom acting this way?" She was thankful for David being at this dinner. He stuck up for her and reminded them that she had suggested countless names, which they had either ridiculed or despised for one reason or another. She was worn out and wanted everyone just to leave. She didn't really like any of them at this moment.

They came into the kitchen just some thirty minutes later, a bit sheepishly, which she enjoyed. Guilt all over their faces at how hard they had been on her. How about Birdie? they asked tentatively, ready for her to blow up.

"I love it!" she shouted. And she did. And that was that. Crisis averted.

She was so grateful that she was alive to see Claire change her minor in French to a major, and become a French professor herself. She had taken the extra steps to get her master's, then her doctorate, and would be a full-time professor soon, teaching at NYU. It was maybe the biggest compliment in her life that Claire, her precious daughter, had followed in her footsteps.

She went up to New York, just to celebrate this decision with Claire. She met her at Buvette in Greenwich Village because it was a darling French restaurant. She walked in and saw Claire seated, perusing the menu. When she looked up and saw Margaret there was disapproval in her gaze.

"Mom, you're dressed like a teenager."

This was not the welcome she was expecting. She felt that sometimes Claire picked an argument with her just to test her unconditional love. They had one of their rare fights because Margaret was dressing as she always did. Heck, Claire had picked these items out! Claire was just in a dark mood. She did not have Margaret's anxieties, but she could get down sometimes and Margaret had often worried about her, as mothers do. She was always on guard, ready to suggest that Claire might want to see a therapist. Her own had been so helpful over the years. Anyhow, the only person she took it out on was her mom, which made Margaret fear that she was bottling all these emotions up. She must have known that Margaret was a safe place, which of course, she was.

They quickly made up as Claire always felt bad when she took her moods out on her mom. Claire took a deep breath and told her she had just broken up with her most recent boyfriend, and even though she didn't even miss him, she missed the thought of him. The attention that came along with having someone.

Margaret's heart ached for her daughter when she was sad. She missed the days when a chocolate milkshake solved everything. Now she had to think, which was much harder. A bit of shopping therapy helped, even though all good therapists advised against it, followed by a hot dog on the street. This was true love, and Claire knew it. Margaret had forbidden all street hotdogs in New York when she found out that the vendors left their carts out overnight and that rats climbed in them during the night to find scraps or just keep warm. Gross! But they were delicious, and Margaret got it down, by focusing on the yumminess and not the rodents.

Claire was in much better spirits when they went to their favourite place in New York, Bemelmans, in the Carlyle Hotel on the Upper East Side. They had to get there early to get a seat, so they were always a bit tipsy by the time the music started, but happy as clams. The music was always outstanding. They weren't sure how they always had someone who had composed music for a famous Broadway play, playing the piano or singing, but there was always someone different and equally talented. But best of all, the entire bar was decorated in scenes from the *Madeline* books by Ludwig Bemelmans. Floor to ceiling, even the lampshades. Everything in those darling pictures. They had been told that in exchange for painting the entire bar, Bemelmans was allowed to live the rest of his life in the penthouse at the top of the Carlyle. It was a great night, one to remember and she was so glad she had gone to visit. Claire had needed her and she had been there for her. She loved when things worked out.

Then, before she knew it, Claire had found someone that she loved dearly. Damn it. She did not want to share her daughter. He was a good man, she had to admit. Which made her say more bad words. He and Margaret just needed time to get to know one another, but if the three of them were in a storm in a little boat in the ocean, it was an easy decision as to who would be thrown overboard first, and she made sure he knew it. Good man or not.

A year later, Claire was pregnant. Margaret launched an all-out search, for the perfect baby name. Every time she was sure they would love one, they shot it down. This sucked too. She wanted input on the baby's name and admittedly they listened politely, at least unless she got too out of control, but in the end, they named their most precious bundle Sophie Margaret, which they knew would make Margaret weep. And it did. When had she become a weeper? Age. It made one more sentimental. Claire told her that it was her husband, Rob's idea. Fine, Margaret felt an unwanted surge of love for the man. That was pretty nice.

And Sophie was a French name. How cool was that. Sophie would be one lucky little girl, because it was clear that Claire would bring her up bilingual. Margaret would get right to work with sticky notes with French words all over the nursery and get on French Amazon to order a stack of baby French books. Oh, and flash cards would be important too. And of course, Tom would help her pick out English books. This time she found herself buying baby Sophie books that she had loved as a child, *The Secret Garden*, *Anne of Green Gables*, *The Railway Children*, *Madeline*, and that little scoundrel *Ramona* — she had loved her spunk. Sophie would be a precocious child, no doubt about it.

In the end, she bought a bookshelf for Sophie's nursery, just so she could claim a shelf for books that she thought Sophie would love when she was older. She always worried she wouldn't be around one day even though her health was perfect, but one never knew; just last week she had had a bad cold and ran to the doctor as she always did, who was very used to seeing her and her 'colds' which might be pneumonia or cholera and written her a prescription for cough syrup because he had been Margaret's doctor forever and he knew that a prescription always 'cured' whatever Margaret had. So, she wrote, in each book, loving notes to her granddaughter, telling her why each book had been special to her. It was a stroke of luck that all three grandkids were so intelligent. Her friends smiled indulgently when she bragged on them.

Actually, she did love Rob, damn it. And Christine too. Rob, bless his heart, made a point of dropping by to visit her regularly, which really was so sweet, and Christine was continually telling Margaret that she couldn't believe what a good mom she had been and how could she ever compare? She was feeding Margaret's ego, and it was pretty successful. Christine marvelled that Margaret had given both kids a menu each night to make a check mark beside the item that they wanted for breakfast the next morning. Granted, she was starting to panic at that stage as the kids were in high school and she was getting close to losing them, so she was starting to baby them. But selfishly, it also made the mornings easier, as neither child was much of a morning person. That way, they could just come downstairs and eat their breakfast and not say a word if they didn't want to. Margaret wasn't sure if Christine thought this was a sweet thing that she had done, or a way too much spoiling kind of thing, but Margaret did not regret these indulgences. She had to sweep away feelings of being replaced and no longer being needed. It sucked, truth be told. She wanted to be the one they turned to, but that stage was over.

Great, her eyes had welled up again. She had been the only one of her friends to not want her children to get married. David told her that was selfish — didn't she want them to be happy? More than anything, she did, she just thought that you didn't have to be married to be happy and she did not want to share them. Claire had told her that she would not marry until she was much older, but then she had gone and done it anyway. Traitor. Margaret never had been good at sharing, but that was her parents' fault. She was an only child and had never had to learn how to share. But seeing her children thriving, even without her, brought her much more joy than it did heartache.

Partie Quatre
La Femme d'un Certain Âge

Paris, France

Chapter 21

Margaret had been living in Paris for several years when she awoke the morning of her sixty-fifth birthday. She had truly never felt better. Why in the world did anyone decide to keep track of people's ages? Wouldn't it be so much better if we didn't know? She felt forty. She felt young. Sure, some parts ached just a bit in the morning, but she could still do everything she wanted. She had a sixty-year-old friend who always told people that she was seventy. Then she enjoyed the looks on their face as they scanned her face and were amazed at how wonderful she looked. But she stopped when someone said she didn't even look sixty-five. Yikes.

Margaret much preferred to lie the other way, and was embarrassed to say that she had done so a few times. She remembered carrying one of her grandchildren into the grocery store and the clerk had asked how old her little boy was. Margaret was so delighted. They thought she was the mother, not the grandmother. She fairly danced out of the store and couldn't wait to tell her mom. But most times, to be fair, they asked if this was her grandchild. Shit. No, Margaret certainly wasn't getting any younger, and yet she felt such a lightness, a *joie de vivre* one could say, that she felt nothing but gratitude to be another year older.

Margaret's neighbours-turned-*amis* had proven to be loyal companions in this foreign city that no longer felt foreign at all. They had arranged a wonderful afternoon picnic in Margaret's honour in her favourite garden in the city — Le Jardin des Tuileries. There would be cheese, bread and real butter. They would have some fantastic red wine and toast to their *santé*. Marie had probably knit her a scarf, which she would wear all winter. There would be gifts from everyone. No French person ever came to a party without a gift. She would receive what she always did. A box of the finest chocolates, a package of macarons from Ladurée, perhaps a tin of tea from Mariage Frère filled with her favourite black tea, and of course flowers, always flowers, always the same colour; whether they were pink or white or salmon coloured, the flowers in the bouquet would be the same colour — so French. If she was lucky, someone would remember that books were her favourite gift, but it would not matter, because she knew there would be a package outside her door from Joseph and Claire and it would be filled with books.

Her bookshelf, once so empty, containing only the twenty books she had brought with her, was now completely filled. Her family had tried over the years to get her to move to something bigger, something nicer, but Margaret would not budge. She loved her neighbourhood, her neighbours and her tiny apartment. George II loved it too. And he was too old to move.

When she was younger, Margaret had approached her birthday with neither dread nor enthusiasm. She didn't love that the number on the scale seemed to creep up with each passing year, or that the crows' feet that appeared when she smiled no longer faded, but instead seemed to sink deeper into the creases of her face.

But her birthday also happened to fall in October, her favourite month of the entire year, the time when, particularly in the northeast, fall was finally in full swing. It was also the one day of the year that she allowed herself to drive to the little Vietnamese restaurant in town and splurge on their classic iced coffee — espresso mixed with sweetened condensed milk. It was five hundred calories of scrumptiousness, and she refused to feel guilty about the indulgence seeing as it was her birthday, after all.

Aside from this one small tradition, she would have preferred if the day came and went without a lot of hoopla. Big parties and surprises gave her anxiety, and too much attention made her uncomfortable. A surprise party would be too much for her and she had always warned friends and family that it really might give her a heart attack and that she would actually hate it. She much preferred small groups of friends and family at dinner to celebrate.

Aside from her social anxiety, she knew that she didn't care much for acknowledging her special day because it always reminded her of her mother's cancer diagnosis. When Margaret was in college, she went home for the weekend of her birthday. Her friends teased her, but she always preferred spending her birthday at home with her parents rather than at some bar surrounded by people. The moment she walked into her parents' house, Margaret could sense that something was off. There was a cake and a little stack of presents, like there was every year, but there was an uneasiness that was palpable. Margaret had always felt that her sensitivity was seen by her parents as a weakness, and they often tiptoed around difficult situations in an attempt to protect her.

"Mom, is everything okay?" she remembered asking shakily. Her parents looked at each other in a telling way. Her father walked over to her, gently explaining that her mother had been diagnosed with breast cancer. Margaret went numb.

"It's very early," she recalled her father saying.

"Sweetie?" her mom was saying. "I'm going to be just fine."

Margaret nodded her head robotically. She felt like she was in a bad dream.

"Really," her mother insisted. "They caught it early. And you know what? I have you to thank."

Margaret still wasn't speaking, but she cocked her head in question.

"I get my mammogram every year in October for you, because it's your birthday month." It was such a beautiful sentiment, yet it made Margaret feel somehow responsible.

Her mother did beautifully in her lumpectomy, calling the whole ordeal, "A blip on the radar," but Margaret still felt uneasy each October.

However, things were beginning to feel different. She was starting to see more clearly, and had begun thinking about how fortunate she was that her mother's cancer was caught early. That it was *her* birthday that inspired her mother to bravely have the exam in the first place. That she too was, at least in this moment, healthy.

For the first time in years, it felt like a day worthy of celebrating. So when Jill asked if she and Rachel could *please* come visit for the big day — they wanted to take her out for a celebratory fancy dinner — she surprised her pal by immediately answering, "Yes!" Jill and Rachel had proved true friends. They were still her best friends even separated by a very large ocean. Margaret had this crazy fantasy that one day Jill and Rachel would move to Paris, and live in her apartment building and they could all be like her crazy aunts had been. She would need a couple tenants to die at just the right time to procure them spots in the building.

Yikes, what a terrible thought. Sometimes her mind still went to a dark place. She really did care for most of the people in her building, but if she were honest, there *were* a few that she hoped would move. They could just sell their apartments to Rachel and Jill. They didn't have to die. The three of them would let themselves become plump on chocolate and croissants and they would drink too much. In fact, they would drink wine at lunch and dinner. Every day. They would stroll the streets arm in arm, and sit in cafés all day. They would take over the apartment building and have wild parties. But her friends still had husbands and jobs in the U.S. and what Margaret cared most about was their happiness. But still, she could dream that maybe one day the stars would align. Their husbands could bum along, she supposed. For now, she basked in the happy thought that they would be coming for a visit soon.

Chapter 22

Margaret took a deep breath of the crisp fall air that surrounded an absolutely picturesque Parisian day. She often wondered if it was normal to feel nostalgic for a moment while it was still happening. When her children were little, she would be putting Joseph to sleep, and he would reach his little hand up, half asleep, and touch her face. Or she and Claire would be in the·car, singing along to the radio, and they would both try to sing louder and sillier than the other until they both had tears running down their cheeks from laughing. These precious flashes in time were so fleeting that, even before they had passed, she felt a pang of sadness amongst the joy, already longing for the moment that she knew would all too soon become the past.

It was how she felt in the autumn, her favourite season. It was so beautiful, but it never seemed to last long enough. With each stiff breeze, more leaves would float to the ground, reminding her that this magical season was already on its way out, once again far too soon. Of course, she knew that the fleetingness of these moments, these seasons, was what made them precious in the first place.

She took another deep breath, remembering the importance of embracing both the joy and the sadness that come with life. On such a beautiful day, there was joy to be found everywhere. She loved how the Parisians embraced the outdoors year-round. Heat, rain, snow, it didn't matter. The French ate or drank outside. She imagined they all had to meet their daily quota of people watching.

She relished the simple decision before her. Which *rue* should she wander down today? *Rue Cler* popped into her head. Yes, today was most definitely a *Rue Cler* kind of day. Located in the 'old money' 7th *arrondissement*, it wasn't a terribly long walk from her apartment. Most people associate the 7th with the Eiffel Tower, the Musée d'Orsay (her favourite museum in Paris) or the Rodin Museum, but she associated it with the fabulous *boulangeries*. Each one was so beautiful that they reminded her of exquisite Fabergé eggs. The only stress was deciding what to order. Summer or winter, there were so many yummy things to eat here.

Perhaps Margaret's favourite part was that she wasn't gaining weight, even though her pastry intake had skyrocketed since moving. She certainly wasn't losing weight either, but walking everywhere seemed to balance out all of the indulgent eating. For the first time in her life, she ate whatever she wanted and didn't feel bad about it. The bread in France also did not give her a stomach ache. There were no preservatives in the bread she bought in the boulangeries. In fact, the bread was rock hard in three to four hours, so it was meant to be eaten right away. That was why she saw Parisians nibbling on their baguette on their way home. And she copied them, and found it highly enjoyable.

Margaret felt a swell of pride each night when she looked at the step counter app on her phone and realized she had walked 15,000, 20,000 or one day even 30,000 steps without even realizing it. She might walk to the Musée d'Orsay, her favourite, and look just at Degas' *Small Dancer*. She had a museum pass now, so she didn't feel guilty if she just spent twenty minutes looking at exactly what she wanted to. She then might walk through the Jardin de Tuileries and after, go find some coffee. It wasn't hard to get exercise in Paris.

It was easy to see where Margaret had gotten her love of travel. So strange to be such a fearful person, yet adventures were so important to Margaret, that she was willing to push through the fear. Joseph was sweet and called it brave. She did not feel brave, but she was grateful that she was stubborn enough that once she set her mind to something, she saw it through, anxieties be damned. Part of the fun was in the journey. She still felt like a kid at Christmas as she left her apartment each day. She settled at Café du Marché at the corner of *Rue Cler* and *Rue du Champ du Mars*, having been told by her landlord that this was one of the neighbourhood's 'hotspots' and a great place to people watch. The people here were fascinating, and she understood why it was considered a national pastime. She felt her cell phone buzz in her crossbody bag, and chuckled to herself as she read a text from David.

'Met any hot Frenchmen yet?'

'Countless!' she replied, still chuckling to herself.

She was so grateful that, after his initial shock, David had been in full support of her decision to take up French in her forties. He had been a true friend over the years. In fact, she suddenly realized that the two had now been friends much longer than they were ever married. When he'd taken the trip to visit her and share the news of his engagement, she'd had one tiny spark of sadness, before she was flooded with happiness for this good man. How kind of him to come tell her in person. It was beyond thoughtful. He was truly her best friend. They talked almost daily now. Their lives were so intertwined with kids and grandkids and they had so much in common. She quickly expressed her concern that David's new wife would not accept their friendship, but he eased her fears by telling her that he had already had a talk with his fiancée that he would not give up his friendship with a woman that he loved as a best friend.

That satisfied Margaret, and after a glamorous dinner that David treated her to at George V, she showed him her favourite spots in Paris. Not the touristy ones. David had seen all of those. She wanted to take him to Le Père Lachaise Cemetery and show him where Jim Morrison was buried, because David had always loved his music. She also just had to take him over to

Victor Hugo's statue on his tomb while they were there, to show him a bump in his trouser line.

"Legend has it that if you place one single flower in his top hat, kiss his lips and rub his excited trouser hump," Margaret told David. "You will forever be granted the perfect husband and amazing bedroom activities, for all eternity." As she had no wish for a husband, nor did David, they passed, but they both laughed and wished him well.

She showed him the only vineyard in Paris, way up in Montmartre and they walked up the hundreds of steps instead of riding the funicular. He had never been to the catacombs of Paris, where six million people are buried right under the Parisian streets, and she had him stand on point zero which is the epicentre of Paris and marks the point of distance to anywhere else in the country. "You're supposed to make a wish while you stand on it," she told him. She made him close his eyes, make a wish and she took a picture, not knowing how much she would treasure it.

And lastly, she had to show him the *Man Stuck in the Wall*, a statue of a man half in and half out of the wall. "It's a French story about a man who discovers that he can walk through walls, but he became too cocky, getting himself stuck in between walls, and to people to this day are still trying to 'pull him out' of the wall. To no avail, obviously," she explained.

David stayed three days and they had a time they would both cherish. Definitely their last time with just the two of them. Their relationship was so safely platonic that he even stayed in her loft. She wasn't so sure that his wife to be would approve of this one bit, but he assured her that his 'bride', who was in her sixties, was confident enough of their relationship that she need not think another thing about it.

Margaret decided that she really liked this woman. And she found out soon after that she did. She was somewhat similar to Margaret, independent yet vulnerable. This woman had that aura. And she was a reader. So Margaret gave her a thumbs up. As David left, he gave her a kiss on the cheek and told her that she was the love of his life, but that he was going to love another woman. Margaret understood exactly what he meant. No one would ever replace David, and that was probably why she remained single. But still, neither regretted their decision to live apart. They were both much happier that way and were able to love each other in a way they couldn't as a married couple. If they had stayed together, the love might have faded and that would have been the real tragedy.

Her heart warmed with joy when she thought about how their ever-expanding family would be visiting her in Paris that year for Christmas, David and his wife, who, thank goodness, Margaret adored; Joseph and his wife with their two precious boys; Claire and her husband and their baby girl. They would love the Christmas markets, where they would find adorable Eiffel Tower ornaments and little glass snow globes.

The Champs-Elysees would be packed with vendors and all sorts of delicious things to eat and drink. She would make sure they went ice-skating at the Grand Palais des Glaces and get all bundled up to take a boat ride down the Seine. She would insist they splurge on a Hermès scarf or a pair of Parisian sunglasses. She would take them to Angelina's for *chocolat chaud* so thick and creamy it would barely pour, and of course pop into Galignani for a book or two, since it was right next door.

Despite the cold, she booked them all on a Fat Bike Tour, one of her favourite touristy things to do. The ride was on completely flat ground, so it was simple enough even for children, who could bike or be pulled in a little buggy behind their parents. There was no boring history lesson on the tour. Instead, as you rode by landmarks, the guide would shout out the most fun and interesting facts. There was always a stop for wine along the way, which was part of the reason for signing up.

And, of course, a trip to Ladurée. Her family would not believe a store could be so beautiful. The macarons were delicate, fragile works of art.

Oh, how would she fit in all the things she wanted to share with them in just a week! She needed to make a list and prioritize. The kids would want to climb to the top of the Arc de Triomphe and take the elevator to the top of the Eiffel Tower. She got out her pencil and paper and wrote 'buy tickets'" She would have to take them to the Louvre, if only to see the *Mona Lisa* and *Winged Victory*, although the kids would probably prefer the room of mummies. Joseph was a bit of a history buff, so she imagined they would leave him in the Louvre all day, whereas the rest of them might stay an hour.

She deeply wished that her mom and dad were coming, but instead her mom had simply requested that they all take a picture with the Charlemagne statue and send it to her. They would also buy a stack of berets for her dad. Her mom loved Paris. She spoke not a word of French, but she had never been intimidated exploring on her own. But they were getting up there in age, and at almost ninety they were doing well, but traveling far from home no longer held the allure it once had. Margaret would make a trip home in the spring for her mom's birthday and stay a couple weeks at their house.

Though they had slightly slowed down in recent months, her parents had come to visit her three times since she'd moved to Paris and stayed for several weeks. She had moved up to the loft and given them her bed. She had pictures all over the walls of the things she and her parents had done together. They always spent time in Paris, but then they would choose a couple places to visit in France. One year, the Loire Valley to see all the amazing castles, another to drink wine in Burgundy. They all loved wine, second only to books. And coffee too, of course. She showed her parents a funny Instagram post of a cup of coffee and a glass of wine, each saying 'She loves me more', 'No, she loves me more'. It made them all laugh because it was so relatable.

They loved their time in Provence. She had made her parents read Peter Mayles' *A Year in Provence* before they visited that year, the first book she had bought when she moved to Paris. They wanted to visit the Luberon region in Provence where Peter had lived and go to all the outdoor markets to buy lavender products, honey and all the spices grown in this breathtakingly beautiful area of France. They all agreed it would be easy to stay there forever.

One year, she took them further south to the Côte d'Azur. It had taken them a bit to get there. There were strikes in Paris, as there frequently were, and no trains were running. Margaret was way too scared to drive them the eight or so hours down to the coast, but her dad stepped up to the plate, rented a car and off they went. The car, of course, had broken down and they had sat by the side of the road for hours before someone finally passed by. Luckily, they had had a couple bottles of wine in the car, so they were having a fine time, and by the time a kind man had stopped to help them, they were calling him 'the best man they had ever known' and asking would he be their friend? He laughed seeing the empty bottles by the road and did his magic under the hood. They had insisted that he have a drink with them, then realized that they had drunk all the wine. He was a good sport, practically patting them on the head and sending them on their way.

They made it in about twelve hours to their hotel in Nice, found a parking place and just ate in the hotel that night, they were so tired.

The next morning, they went to go check on their car but it wasn't there. Going back into the hotel *le hotelier* informed them that they had parked in a no parking zone. This was not good, he told them. "Is very difficult to get your car back. And *très cher*."

Great. He sure was right. They spent the day going from one bureaucrat to another. Paperwork had to be stamped, then they were sent to the next office who had to check that they were who they said they were, then back to the original office with a stamped paper saying that yes, they were who they said they were. When, finally, hours later, they pulled up in a taxi to the 'place where bad people's cars are', it was afternoon. Nobody was having much fun, as there were some leftover headaches from yesterday.

When *l'homme* (the man) at the lot said that they were missing a stamp, that no he could under no circumstance release their car without the proper stamps, Margaret stepped up with a hundred Euros, and he gladly opened the gate. But where was their car? "Oh, madame, I gave that car to someone else this morning. But not to worry, you may take another car." He led them over to, wait, what was this miniature vehicle? It looked like a clown's car. But beggars can't be choosy. They tried to look sincere when they thanked the man for the exchange of an SUV for a toy car. At least it was easy to park, once they found the right place.

They had loved Nice, though, and taken time to go up into the charming town of Saint Paul de Vence, where they had the most delicious lunch and the most gorgeous views of the Mediterranean. Her mother loaded up on French products and when they had had enough of the place where the rich and famous go to see and be seen, they headed back to Paris in their mini car, all of their knees up to their chests for eight hours. But again, as is usually the case, later it became a funny story to tell.

Margaret smiled, thinking of her precious parents. She had decided to splurge and buy an Hermès scarf for her mom this Christmas. It was by far the most expensive scarf she had ever bought. She would send it back with Claire, who would make sure she got it. And she would let Joseph and Claire pick out their Christmas gifts in Paris, and of course she would take the little ones to the finest toy store in Paris and let them go wild.

Thinking of her loved ones all together, in this magical city during the most splendid time of the year, Margaret was completely lost in a warm and fuzzy daydream. After her delicious coffee and *pain au chocolat*, she would stroll through the gardens of the Rodin Museum, which was famous for Rodin's sculpture, *The Thinker*. She might pull a book out of her purse and sit under a tree in the gardens, reading and occasionally looking up to admire the view. This life she was living was making her grateful for every single moment. She carried a little Moleskin notebook in her purse that served as a catchall for all of her thoughts. She packed it with her ideas, her grocery lists, great quotes she read, and most of all, the things she was thankful for. Margaret used to keep everything neatly organized on her cell phone, but she so preferred an old-fashioned pen and paper. Always a leather notebook which fit in her purse. She began to write, getting completely lost in her thoughts.

She only looked up upon hearing a man rather loudly clear his throat. "I'm so sorry to bother you, madame," the man said politely. "I heard that there was an American professor and tutor who lived in the area, and I was hoping you might be willing to offer me French lessons."

He looked about her age and it was clear he was handsome in his day. He wore jeans and a fisherman's sweater with the sleeves pushed up, and Margaret couldn't help but notice that he had on a brand-new pair of sneakers. Men here wouldn't be caught dead wearing running sneakers with jeans, but Margaret found it endearing. It reminded her of something her dad would have worn, and she instantly imagined that perhaps one of his children had bought them for him, wanting him to be comfortable as he walked around Paris.

Nevertheless, she was certain he would be an awful pupil. Perhaps she could pawn him off on one of the younger tutors she had gotten to know.

"I'm sorry, these days I really only take on serious students," Margaret said with a shrug.

"Oh, I assure you I am very serious!" the man chirped enthusiastically. "My wife, well, my late wife, she always wanted us to take up French. And well, you know how the story goes; we just never got around to it."

Margaret's face softened.

"Anyway, I've been here for five weeks and still haven't got a damn clue how to order my breakfast, let alone hire a contractor to help fix up my place. My kids think I'm nuts for buying a run-down apartment in Paris, but my wife would have loved it," the man said, smiling wistfully. "Plus," he continued, "I've gotten spunkier with age."

"You know, so have I," Margaret said, a smile starting to form on her lips.

"It's funny how that happens," the man replied.

"All right then," she agreed, gesturing for the man to have a seat. "*Commençons.*"

Let's begin.

CPSIA information can be obtained
at www.ICGtesting.com
Printed in the USA
BVHW040259300722
643335BV00001B/3

9 781800 164062